DAWN

SHADOWS OF THE VOID BOOK 3

J.J. GREEN

INFINITEBOOK

BOOK ORDER

The Books of Shadows of the Void - Complete Series

Prequel: Starbound
Book 1: Generation
Book 2: Stranded
Book 3: Dawn
Book 4: Shadowrise
Book 5: Underworld
Book 6: Burned
Book 7: Trapped
Book 8: Mars Born
Book 9: Shadow Battle
Book 10: Shadow War
Books 1 - 3 The Galathea Chronicles
Books 4 - 7 The Earth Chronicles
Books 8 - 10 The Galactic Chronicles

1

———

Arriving from a starjump was like swimming up from deep water, emerging into the air, and rising to the upper stratosphere. Carl had starjumped more times than he could remember, but he didn't think he'd ever get used to it. Intense pressure on his body and, it seemed, his mind, gave way to a sense of infinite space and incredible lightness. Like the rest of the crew on the bridge of the *Galathea*, he grabbed the nearest fixed object as if to steady himself, even though he was well-secured in his pilot's harness.

The first thing he did was check on Harrington, who was sitting bound to a seat at the comm console. She was looking a little green, but she seemed okay. That misborn Haggardy was taking his revenge too far. Harrington had done the right thing when she'd put him in the brig. What else was the chief security officer supposed to do if she suspected he'd been infected by a hostile alien? As far as Carl was concerned, Haggardy was still under suspicion.

Turning his gaze to the former First Mate Haggardy, now acting master of the *Galathea*, he had an urge to punch the older man in his smug, self-satisfied face. What had he done to protect the crew from the aliens on K. 67092d? Nothing. It had been up to Harrington, Navigator Sayen Lee, and himself to save the ship and their shipmates. Now, the *Galathea* had lost nearly twenty officers, and their prospecting mission for their employer, Polestar, was over. No one would receive any bonuses. The crew was on the verge of mutiny, and it was possible one of them could be possessed by an alien.

"Not bad, Lingiari," said Haggardy, releasing his safety harness, standing, and stretching. "Grantwise couldn't have done better himself."

Carl grimaced. As far as he was concerned, if it weren't for Haggardy's spinelessness, Pilot Grantwise might still be alive. Carl had always longed to pilot a starship, but not like this.

The comm console bleeped. It hadn't taken the governorship of Dawn—the planet they were now orbiting—long to get in touch. Haggardy went over to the panel and swiped and pressed the screen. After briefly scanning the message, he commanded the two defense units who stood guarding the door, and who accompanied him everywhere round the clock, to follow him as he left the bridge.

Carl unclipped his harness and went to Harrington. He unknotted the binding around her ankles and wrists.

"Thanks," she said, "but are you sure you should do this? He could be back any minute."

"Krat him. What's he going to do? Tie you up again?"

"He could put me in the brig, or worse."

"If he puts you in the brig, at least you'll get to lie down. And as for doing anything worse, that'd take guts. Does that sound like Haggardy to you?"

"You've got a point." Harrington rose to her feet and

twisted her ankles and wrists in circles. She was half a head taller than Carl, but that had never bothered him. He'd always liked her statuesque frame.

Harrington returned to the comm seat and scanned the screen. "He's taking the call from Dawn in his cabin. I wonder what they're talking about."

"I'm wondering how he's going to spin what happened on K. 67092d to make himself come out smelling sweet," said Carl. "That'll be a job and a half."

"What's he going to tell them about you and me, and Lee?" Harrington shook her head. "It's going to be hard to explain ourselves to Polestar and maybe the Global Government when we don't know the story he's told them."

"No point in worrying about it now." Carl perched on the comm console. "So, what's the plan?"

"I'm waiting to hear what the governor of Dawn has to say. Why did Polestar tell us to come here and not return to Earth for quarantine? We have to be sure none of the remaining crew are infected before we go planetside anywhere in the galaxy. We can't risk those aliens spreading." She thumbed an icon on the comm screen, but it had no effect. "I can't access external comms. I bet we're both locked out of all but the most basic systems. If we get the chance, we have to warn the governor about Haggardy. If only I could contact Dawn directly myself, or even Earth."

The door to the bridge opened, and Haggardy returned. "I don't recall telling you to untie our security officer, Lingiari."

"I don't remember you having any reason to tie her up."

Haggardy's eyebrows rose. "You must have a short memory, then. But never mind. Luckily for you, you've pre-empted my order. I was about to set you free myself, Harrington."

"Came to your senses, finally?" the security officer asked. "Or maybe that alien you're carrying around messed with your brain?"

The acting master's expression hardened. "That's a serious accusation to be throwing around. I'd be careful about repeating it to the governor when you arrive on Dawn. Or you might find yourself under suspicion."

"You're sending her to Dawn?" asked Carl.

"I'm sending both of you. Or rather, the governor has requested that you pay her a visit."

Carl and Harrington's gazes met.

"She would have liked to speak to Navigator Lee, too, but that would be difficult to arrange with the navigator in stasis. The governor's an understanding woman, and she agreed to leave her out of investigations for the time being, until the ship is declared free of infection and safe for her to board."

"But Lingiari and I could be infected," Harrington said. "How does she know we won't spread the infection to Dawn?"

"Dawn is a quarantine and vetting station for ships that might be harboring this infection," replied Haggardy. "The governor explained that it isn't the first time this hostile species has been encountered. Polestar recognized the pattern of events we experienced, and that's why it sent us here. You'll both be tested. If you pass, you'll wait planetside until the whole ship's crew has been examined and cleared. Then, we can return to Earth."

Carl couldn't see how it would be possible to test for something so difficult to detect. He wondered how many false positives they'd found. "And if we don't pass?"

"I've sent a team of defense units to clear the shuttle wreckage from the shuttle bay," said Haggardy. "A transport from Dawn will be arriving soon. You can go there to wait for it. Don't even think about trying anything, Harrington. I can countermand the defense units in a moment, and even if you were to get back control of the ship, where do you think you would go?"

Haggardy obviously wasn't going to tell them what would happen if they weren't cleared of carrying the alien infection. And what did he mean when he said the species had already been encountered? Was it already spreading across the galaxy?

The ship's corridors were quiet as they went to the shuttle bay. The crew were always subdued after arriving from a starjump, and Carl imagined that many were confused and worried by the events leading up to their arrival on Dawn. Like him, they'd probably anticipated a return to Earth, not this detour.

At the bay, the sight of the remains of the small ship he'd flown on countless trips to and from the *Galathea* tore at Carl's heart. The moment that he'd participated in its destruction had been a sad one.

Defense units were busy pulling apart the wreckage and taking it away. Where parts of the shuttle had melted to the floor, they were using their weapons to sever them.

Harrington leaned against the shuttle bay wall, her arms folded.

"We're just going to do what he says?" Carl asked.

"I don't see what choice we have. He's right. We can't do anything while he has the defense units under his control. If we run and hide, they'll find us in the end, and we'd only be putting off the inevitable. Besides, we aren't infected, so we'll pass the tests, and then maybe we'll get a chance to tell our side of the story. And if Haggardy's possessed, they'll find out."

"I'm wondering what else the governor said that he didn't tell us," said Carl.

"Yeah, I'm wondering that too. Hey, Is Flux going to be okay while we're gone?"

Carl had been concerned about his small alien friend, too. "Yeah, he'll be fine. The little fella's got plenty of friends to look after him." Carl smiled at the memory of finding out that Flux hadn't been as much of a secret aboard ship as he'd thought he had.

An alarm sounded, and the shuttle bay lights flashed. A synthetic voice came over the intercom, warning them to evacuate as a transport was approaching. Carl and Harrington waited outside the bay while the transport docked. When they returned, a small, neat, kite-shaped shuttle awaited them. An MT11. It was an old model, but Carl had always appreciated the economy and simplicity of its design.

As they boarded, he noticed a modification: a plexiglass screen separated the passengers from the pilot. A precautionary measure, Carl guessed, to protect the pilot from infection.

They strapped themselves in, and Carl tried to recall what he knew of the place they were going. All he could remember about Dawn was that it was a frontier colony: a resource-rich but undeveloped world that the Global Government had purchased for a fortune from Polestar's rival prospecting company. The Government had strongly encouraged a disaffected group who were generating political tensions to settle there. What had they been called? He couldn't remember.

Dawn was also the only planet where humans had settled alongside a secondary colonizing alien species, the Haidiren.

"What do you think's going to happen if we don't pass the test?" he asked Harrington.

"Why wouldn't we pass?" But from the way she didn't look him in the eye, Carl guessed she was thinking the same thing as him—what if the whole thing was a set up to get them off the ship quickly and quietly? What if there was no test? What might really be awaiting them on Dawn?

2

———

The shuttle doors opened, and Jas Harrington unexpectedly got her first close-up glimpse of Dawn. She'd thought there would be some kind of sealed tunnel leading them from the shuttle to the testing center, something to keep them separate to prevent the spread of any infection they might be carrying. What she saw instead, beyond the shuttle runway and perimeter fence, were undulating hills of some kind of mossy material the color of copper. It was a warm, fresh hue, and the air that swept into the shuttle was fresher still, fresh and humid, and had a light scent unlike anything Jas had encountered.

Armed guards appeared at the bottom of the shuttle ramp, and Jas and Lingiari followed them down the runway to a low, white building that looked like it'd been built from a kit, as it probably had. No other shuttlecraft could be seen, though there was a small hangar.

If the governor of Dawn was planning on bringing the crew down for testing two by two, Jas and Lingiari would be there for quite some time.

Inside the white building, they were separated into different rooms. A man in medic's clothes greeted Jas and asked her to lie down on a bed that slid inside a whole body scanner. The man then took urine, blood, saliva, and hair samples from her. Finally, he clipped a device to her finger and asked her a long battery of questions about her childhood, home life, relationships, career, and other life experiences, all the while watching a screen she couldn't see. At some of Jas's answers, such as how she'd grown up in a government institution, how she didn't have any close friends, and how her idea of a relaxing day off was target practice, the man raised his eyebrows.

After several hours, her tests were over. He handed her a few pieces of some kind of printed paper. The Dawn settlement certainly was basic. "You're fine. You gave some surprising answers, but you're human."

Muscles that Jas didn't know she'd been tensing relaxed. She got up, and the man directed her to another room, where she found an older woman sitting at a desk. Jas wondered what had happened to Lingiari.

"Welcome to Dawn," the woman said and gestured to Jas to sit. "You must be C.S.O. Harrington. Your acting master informed me about you."

"Where's the man I came with? Pilot Lingiari?" Jas remained standing.

"I understand your caution, but please don't be concerned. Your colleague also isn't a Shadow. He passed all the tests quickly. He's already gone into town. I wanted to speak to you both about the infection process and to reassure you."

"A Shadow? Is that what you call people possessed by the aliens? You know what the infection is?"

"Yes, we have some ideas. I'm Governor Siam, but you can call me Sashquita."

"You're the governor?" exclaimed Jas. She'd thought this woman was some kind of doctor.

"That's right. You were probably expecting someone a little more formal, right?" She smiled. "Please sit down, and I'll explain." When Jas complied, she continued, "Dawn's just an end-of-the-galaxy colony planet. We're pretty laid back around here. Most of us are working hard just to survive. We don't have much time or patience for formalities.

"It seems like this is the first you've heard of Shadows? That's not surprising. The Global Government isn't exactly broadcasting the news. Aliens who look identical to the people they've killed?" She shook her head. "You can't really blame them for wanting to keep it quiet. Who's to know if a friend or relative is really who you think they are, or if they're an alien? By the way, you'll be required to sign a non-disclosure agreement before you return to—"

"Wait," said Jas. "What do you mean? I thought the aliens infected people...got inside them somehow and took over their minds. You're telling me they clone their victims and then kill them?"

"That's right. It's easy to misunderstand. For a long time, the Global Government also thought the aliens were only possessing their victims. But no, the alien only *looks like* the person they killed. That's why they're called Shadows. They're like dark copies of the original. The aliens seem to read the DNA of anyone who gets caught in one of their traps, then they destroy the subject and appear as his or her copy, housing all the original memories and knowledge. But the personality is that of the alien."

Jas sat back in her chair. It was a lot to take in. "These

Shadows, they look and sound the same as their victims. Is the DNA the same? If so, how can you tell them apart from the original?"

"I'd rather not tell you that right now," said the governor. "I hope you understand."

"Can you tell me why Lingiari finished earlier than me?"

Governor Siam paused a moment before answering, "The main difficulty we have with testing is, from what we've seen, that the mind copying they do means a lot of the original personality is there. It can take a while to sort out the human from the Shadow's traits. Some scientists think the Shadow itself can get confused as to who it really is after spending a long time living as a clone.

"But don't be alarmed. You've already passed." She paused and looked down at her hands for a moment before continuing. "Your acting master informed me of what happened aboard your ship. What I told your shipmate, and what I wanted to tell you, is that you can rest assured that our testing is effective. I know you harbor suspicions toward Acting Master Haggardy. But for the sake of harmony and—if I might say—your own career, you would be wise to drop them." She stood.

"I wish you an enjoyable stay on Dawn, C.S.O. Harrington. Now, if you follow the guard, he'll take you to your transportation."

"Wait. What about the Shadows you identify? What happens to them?"

But the governor only pursed her lips and shook her head slightly.

As Jas was shown to the exit, she recalled the number of alien structures she'd visited on K. 67092d. Shadow traps. She'd been inside twelve while securing the resource assessment sites, and another when the *Galathea* had crash-landed on the planet. Thirteen. Thirteen opportunities to leave her DNA. Was she in fact a Shadow and she'd forgotten it? Was Lingiari?

At the outer door, a guard told her, "You've got ID, some money, and an accommodation chit. If you follow the road, around the bend you'll find transportation. It's pre-programmed to take you into town. Just one road, and just one town. It's impossible to get lost around here."

"Where do I go to sleep?"

"There just one—"

"Place to stay. I get it." Her visit to Dawn didn't look like it was going to be very interesting.

Jas quickly found the single-seater vehicles. Small and boxy, they had space for luggage at the back. She tried a door, and when it opened she got inside. The vehicles were similar to all-terrain buggies she'd driven when she'd been at training college in Antarctica. They were wide-wheeled and high-carriaged, as if designed for off-road driving. But the controls on this vehicle were set with only two destinations: Dawntown/Shuttle Base. She pressed Dawntown. *Dawntown?* The settlers of new worlds were always so unimaginative. The machine started up and moved off without any further operation.

It wasn't far to the capital of Dawn. About twenty kilometers away, it was hidden among low, rolling hills. Like the shuttle base, some of the buildings were low, pre-fabricated structures. Others were made of some kind of dried mud or rammed earth, and these were a range of dun colors.

Jas passed the simple houses. There didn't seem to be any shops, and if there were any factories they were undistinguishable. Only one building was three-story. It was on the edge of town, but must have been visible from everywhere due to its height. Jas was surprised how undeveloped the place was. She was sure this colony was at least a couple of decades old. Had they really only managed to build one town on an entire planet?

She attracted the attention of everyone she passed, and small children ran after the slow-moving, one-person car. It pulled into a bay next to some others and stopped. Jas got out. Lingiari was nowhere to be seen. Feeling disappointed that the pilot hadn't waited for her, she set off down a street that had some kind of marketplace at the end of it. She hoped someone would be there who could tell her where she was supposed to sleep.

When Jas was about halfway down the street, a teenage boy appeared at the end, running in her direction. He was longhaired, scruffy, and had the beginnings of a mustache and beard shadowing his lips. As he got closer, two men appeared behind him, running after him. She recognized their uniforms. They belonged to the army of the Global Government. Jas didn't want to get involved in Dawn's affairs, so she stepped to one side to give all three of them plenty of room to pass, but the kid had spotted her. He changed course. He was heading straight for her.

He was about seventeen, she guessed. His hair was wavy and brown, and he was dressed in simple clothes made of coarse-woven, natural materials. That was all she had time to notice before he reached her.

Grabbing both of her arms, the kid exclaimed, "Take me away with you on your ship. I'll do anything you want. Please."

3

A second later, the men who were chasing the kid caught up and pulled him away from Jas. They were a lieutenant and a private. The soldiers wrestled with the kid, who fought their attempts to restrain him. "Hey," exclaimed Jas as he went sprawling. The private hauled him roughly to his feet.

The kid continued to struggle. "Let me go. I don't want to go back there. I'm not going home, and you can't make me."

"Huh, we'll see about that," said the private. He pushed the kid against the wall and pulled his hands behind his back. He gasped in pain.

"Take it easy, Trip," said the lieutenant to the private. He went over to the struggling boy. "Look, Makey, don't make it harder on yourself. We have to take you back home. *You* know it. We know it. There's nothing anyone can do about it. If you fight, the only person who's going to get hurt is you."

Makey's arms went limp. The soldier holding him slipped handcuffs around his wrists. His head fell forward, and his shoulders sagged. He averted his head, but Jas could hear quiet sobs.

"You're only taking him home?" asked Jas. "You aren't arresting him?" The kid seemed to be overreacting a little.

"Yep, just taking him back to his mom and dad. Running away from home isn't a crime." The lieutenant paused and looked at Jas. He was tall and broad-shouldered. His hair was black and his eyes were nearly the same color. The man clearly kept himself in shape. "You want to walk down with us? You're off that quarantined starship, aren't you? I can show you to the hostel. It isn't far, and it's on our way."

"Uh, okay. Thanks."

"I'm Lieutenant Theron," said the man as they walked, "but you can call me Idris. This over-zealous young soldier is Private Trip Cassady."

"Pleased to make your acquaintance, ma'am." The private had a firm grip on young Makey's arm as they went ahead of Jas and the lieutenant. The boy was sniffing and trying to wipe off the snot hanging from his nose with his shoulder.

"Are you the first off your ship?" asked Idris.

"Yes, me and the pilot. But I don't know where he's gone. I'm Jas Harrington. Security officer."

"Security officer? We're in the same line of business, just about. I thought you might be in security from the look of your uniform. Polestar, isn't it?"

"That's right. But my clothes are a little warm for this climate. They're better suited to a starship owned by a company on a fuel-economy drive. I was hoping I could pick up something cooler here. They gave me some paper money, but I don't know how much things cost."

"I know how much you've been given. All the crews they test get the same amount. You should be able to buy a change of clothes with that. There are a few stalls selling clothes here."

They'd arrived at the market, which consisted of only a dozen or so stalls. Three sold clothes, all very rough, simple and similar to what Makey was wearing. Other stalls sold fruit and vegetables and dried beans. One sold simple woven baskets and earthenware bowls and plates.

"I can give you directions to the hostel if you want to stop here and buy clothes," said Idris.

"No, it's okay. I'll make my way back later." She was wondering if Lingiari was waiting for her at the hostel.

"Don't leave it too late," said Idris. "They begin to pack up about half an hour before sunset. No street lights, you see."

Dawn really was the back of beyond.

Private Trip and Makey had drawn a little way ahead of Jas and the lieutenant. She leaned over to speak softly to Idris. "Don't you think it's strange that the boy doesn't want to go home? Before you caught up to him, he was asking for passage on my starship."

Idris grimaced. "I'm sorry to say I don't find it strange at all. Or maybe I should say, not unusual. One thing you've got to understand about the people of this place is that they all belong to a sect. They came to Dawn to live according to their principles. Or more accurately the Global Government heavily persuaded them to come here.

"You could put down Makey's attitude to isolation and a hard life, with nothing more to do than work the family farm day after day. But frankly, the people are so insular and strange sometimes, I wonder what goes on behind closed doors.

"I'd like to help these kids, I really would. But the most I can do is to take them home to their families, where at least they've got food in their stomachs and a place to sleep. It's better than being out on the streets. Believe me, none of them would last long out on their own. There's no safety net here."

"Why doesn't the governor do something?" asked Jas. "Surely that's her job?"

"Huh. *Dawn—a new beginning, a new life for all.* That was the Global Government slogan. Now, how embarrassing would it be for the government if it got out what a miserable hole for misborns Dawn is? The governor keeps up appearances, or she's out of a job."

"Krat." Jas's eyes lingered on the skinny boy walking ahead of her. What a life. She knew only too well what a miserable existence some children led, despite humanity's supposedly great advances. There hadn't been much in the way of reductions in human suffering and cruelty.

"What's the army doing here?" she asked Idris. "There don't seem to be enough people to warrant peace-keeping forces."

"Ah, here we are," he said. stopping. They were outside one of the few two-story buildings in town. It was wide and had two wings stretching back from the road. All the windows were shuttered. "Sorry, I would answer your question, but I have to take this boy home. I'll explain why the army's on Dawn another time, if you like."

"Uh, okay."

The lieutenant smiled, and Jas's stomach tingled. Her gaze went from his even, white teeth to his eyes, which returned the too-long look. "See you another time," she said.

As he moved away with Trip and Makey, her gaze lingered on him for a moment before she went inside the hostel.

She gave the woman behind the counter her accommodation chit and received a simple metal key with a room number on it. She went upstairs and unlocked the door of her room with the key. She felt like she'd traveled back in time and wondered if she would have to light an oil lamp when the sun went down.

Inside, the room was a weird mixture of modern and rustic. She checked out the bed. Metal-framed with a mattress that was the standard mold-to-your-body type, it had clearly arrived on a colony ship. Spread over the mattress were rough sheets and blankets made of a natural thread. The pillow seemed to be stuffed with genuine feathers. The room had no comm, no screens or interfaces, nor any other electronic devices. There was a light strip at least, and from the gentle hum she could hear, the electricity for it came from a generator nearby.

Jas went to the window, pushed the shutters open, and looked out over the low roofs of Dawntown. She wondered where Lingiari was. She should have asked the receptionist which room the pilot was in. Beyond the town, the sun was nearing the hilly horizon. She would have to hurry if she wanted to buy some clothes before the market closed. She was uncomfortably hot and sweaty, and she didn't relish the idea of wearing her uniform for another day.

Returning to the market at a fast pace, Jas managed to catch the owner of a clothing stall as he was taking the last of his items down. He had little to offer that would fit Jas. In the end, she had to settle on some men's trousers that fit her round the hips but ended halfway up her calves, and a baggy tunic. She bought a woven belt to pull in the tunic.

By the time Jas arrived back at the hostel, Dawn's sun had swiftly set, and darkness had fallen like a cloak. She had to navigate the streets with the help of light shining through slatted shutters.

When she found the door of the hostel, she went in and

asked the receptionist which room the *Galathea's* pilot was staying in. It turned out Lingiari was her neighbor, but when she knocked on his door, he didn't answer. She tried again. Either Lingiari had gone out or he was sound asleep. If it was the latter, she didn't want to wake him. She would wait until morning.

4

———

Makey was cutting grass, dragging the cutter over the undulating ground, slicing the plants just above their roots. They called it grass, but Makey knew from reading the forbidden school books that it wasn't like the grass of Earth, and that they only called it so because its growing point was just above the root, the same as its namesake, and not near the shoot-tip like most plants. This meant it could be harvested again and again, as long as the soil sustained it.

"Where were you running to, Makey?" asked Neeve, his sister, as she walked behind the cutter, raking the cut stalks together.

Where Makey was harnessed to the cutter, the straps cut into the welts his father had inflicted with a cane, after the soldiers had brought him home.

"Makey?" Neeve repeated. His sister was five years younger than him, and often annoying, but of all the things he tolerated in his hard life, he minded her the least.

"I don't know. Away. Somewhere away from here."

"Da was so angry when he knew you'd gone, he threw a plate against the wall. Mam and me stayed out of his way."

"I'm sorry."

"It was no matter. I hid in the cellar till I heard him go out to look for you."

Makey grimaced and pulled harder against his harness, feeling the pain was a justified punishment for the trouble he'd caused Mam and his sister. He'd never meant for them to suffer. The extra speed he put on caused the cutter to slip and then jam, stopping him sharply and causing him to stagger.

"There it goes again. Always sticking," Neeve said lightly.

Makey slipped off the harness and knelt to free the cutter. Copper stalks were wound around the rotary blades. Stripped of their outer skins, they oozed red sap. Makey began gingerly picking out the trapped vegetation, but his mind was elsewhere, and before long he'd cut his thumb. Drops of blood flowed out and mixed with the sticky sap.

"Ow," he exclaimed. He sat back on his heels and sucked his thumb.

Neeve dropped her rake and ran to her brother's side. "Have you cut yourself? Can I see?"

"No, it's okay. It'll stop bleeding in a moment."

His sister raised a hand to the sky and said, "Earth Mother, hear me—"

"Stop it, Neeve. I don't want to hear that nonsense. I hear enough of it at home."

Closing her eyes, the girl continued, "Bring healing to my brother. Make him whole and as perfect as you are, I beseech you."

Makey rolled his eyes. He took his thumb out of his mouth. The bleeding was slowing down. A single drop oozed slowly to the surface.

Neeve also looked at his thumb. "You see, Makey? It worked. Earth Mother is making your thumb better."

"No, she isn't. It's getting better by itself."

"No, it's Earth Mother. If I hadn't said the prayer, your thumb wouldn't have stopped bleeding."

"Yes, it would. I know it would, Neeve. I've tried it. When I've been alone, I didn't ask Earth Mother's help, and my cuts got better by themselves."

Neeve shook her head. "That just shows how loved you are, Makey. Someone, somewhere was saying a prayer for you. Others care about you, and they ask Earth Mother for her protection for you, even if you don't."

His conscience twinged. This was Neeve's way of reproaching him for running away and leaving her.

"Neeve, I..." He gestured for her to sit next to him. "When I left home yesterday, I saw a spacewoman in town. She was very tall, and she was wearing a starship uniform. There's a starship above Dawn right now, orbiting the planet. Did you know that?"

Her eyes fixed on her brother's face, Neeve slowly shook her head.

"No, because they didn't tell us, did they? Not Da or Mam, or Teacher Clary. There are lots of things they don't tell us. We see these people from other planets some times, but we're not supposed to talk about them."

"Neeve, I have a secret to tell you, but you mustn't tell Da or Mam, okay?"

"All right," his sister replied doubtfully.

"You know I have to clean the school every night as punishment for asking too many questions in class?"

Neeve nodded, her eyes fixed on her brother.

"I found a cupboard that was locked, and when I broke it open, there were lots of books inside. School books that we never use in class. I've read some of them, and the information in there is different from what Teacher Clary tells us. Nothing in those books says that Earth Mother chose us to come to Dawn as the last step before Heaven. They talk about a group called Green Earthers."

A crease appeared between his sister's brows.

"The books say that Green Earthers believe in Earth Mother," continued Makey, "who bestows health and well-being on her followers, providing they live naturally—no artificial chemicals, everything made by hand from natural materials, all food cooked at home from whole ingredients. They believe that nothing bad will happen to you if you follow Earth Mother's rules, and that when you die, you become part of the natural cosmos."

"Makey, what are you talking about? That isn't anything strange, that's the truth."

He sighed. "Is it the truth, or is it just what some people believe? Don't you think that the Green Earthers sound exactly like us and all the other families we know? Only we don't call ourselves Green Earthers anymore because aren't on Earth, we're on Dawn. And we don't have to give ourselves a name because we aren't a separate group; we're the majority here. On Dawn, being a Green Earther just means you're the same as most people.

"It's like our parents brought those books to Dawn to teach us about our group, but then they decided to ignore what had happened in the past and pretend there was only ever one way of thinking about things, that there *is* only one way of thinking about things."

Neeve got to her feet. "Even if there is something in what you read, even if Da and Mam were Green Earthers before they came here, why does it matter? What's wrong with the way we live?" She brushed grass stalks from her knees.

"Why aren't you happy, Makey? Why do you want to leave us?" Her voice wobbled as if she were about to cry, and she turned her head away.

A lump rose in Makey's throat as he bent over the cutter once more and pulled free the last of the stalks. "I can't be happy. I've tried. I've tried to do my chores, say my prayers, and be a good son and brother, but it isn't enough. I can't believe this is the best way to live until I've seen the alternatives. I have to find out what else they haven't told us. I want to go to Earth and see other planets."

"But we need you," blurted Neeve. "Who'll cut the grass? Who'll hang it to dry? Who'll help weave it if you go?"

"I don't know, but I can't help it. I have to find things out for myself. I feel like if I stay here any longer, I'm going to die, just the same as if these stalks wound around my throat while I was sleeping and choked me."

Neeve stomped over to her rake, picked it up, and began to violently rake the cut grass. "It's a curse you've brought on yourself, this feeling. It's your own fault. You turned away from the Earth Mother. You don't say your prayers. I know you don't. I never hear you at night, and at the table, you just move your lips without speaking. And now Earth Mother's turned her back on you. That's why you don't want to be here anymore. If you would just start praying again, everything would be okay. You wouldn't want to leave us."

"Neeve, it isn't that, and I don't want to leave you. Not you, anyway. Why don't you come with me? We could escape together, and we could find out the truth for ourselves."

"You'd better start cutting again," replied his sister. "We haven't done much, and Da will be angry." Her face was set, but Makey thought she also looked a little frightened.

"All right." He lifted the harness and slipped it over his

head. He'd been the same at Neeve's age. It was only in the last couple of years that Makey had questioned the lifestyle they led and the things his parents had told him. He would have reacted the same as Neeve if anyone had suggested anything different, not so long ago. He didn't know how to convince his sister.

He began to pull the cutter again. In front of him stretched a rolling sea of copper. At that moment, it looked to him like a representation of his life on Dawn. Featureless, monotonous, and unending.

His entire being rebelled against the prospect. He had to leave. He simply had to, though there was nowhere for him to go. He would run away again, tonight, as soon as everyone was asleep. He would head out into the wild and try to make a life for himself there. And if he died, it wouldn't matter. It would be a quicker death than the one he was currently living.

5

Lieutenant Idris Theron led Jas into the army barracks. The sentry checked her ID and gave her a cursory once-over with his eyes as they passed through the gate. Jas wondered what a sight she must look in her poorly made, shapeless pants and tunic, but at least the air could now circulate over her skin and cool her down.

There had been no answer at Lingiari's door that morning, and Jas was beginning to become concerned about the AWOL pilot. She'd asked the woman at the hostel desk if she'd seen him come in the night before, but she hadn't. That didn't mean much, however, because it wasn't necessary to pass the desk to go up to the rooms. It was conceivable that Lingiari was simply catching up on lost sleep after the recent harrowing few days aboard the *Galathea*.

"How was breakfast?" asked Idris Theron.

Jas grimaced. "Interesting."

The lieutenant laughed. "Don't tell me, seaweed soup and crackers? It's the cheapest food available here. And, no, those crackers aren't made from wheatflour."

"Do I want to know what they're made from?"

"Probably not. But if you're still hungry, our army food is a little better tasting...?"

"I wouldn't say no to a second breakfast." Jas's stomach rumbled, and she wasn't sure if it was from hunger or the after-effects of the green, salty soup she had forced into it.

They went into the canteen, where the cook was in the process of closing up the kitchen. Lieutenant Theron's disarming smile worked its magic on the man, and he warmed up some beans and hash browns. Jas's heart skipped a beat when Idris placed a mug of a steaming dark brown liquid in front of her. She leaned forward and inhaled. Her eyes widened. "It isn't...It can't be?"

"It's real coffee. Taste it."

Jas took a sip and closed her eyes as the liquid slipped down her throat. "It's amazing. I haven't drunk real coffee in years. I didn't know life was so comfortable in the military. I'm in the wrong job."

"We need some compensation for working on remote planets at the ends of the galaxy. There are plenty of vacancies, if you're serious."

Shrugging as she took another sip of the delicious liquid, Jas said, "I don't know. I'm not much of a team player. I prefer it with just me and my units."

"Ah, defense units. We have some divisions of them in the army. I've never worked with them close up, though. What are they like?"

"Hmmm...they're kinda like big, dumb, killing machines. Or that's how they seem at first, anyway. Until you're used to them and their little ways, they're pretty scary. But there's something about them..." She paused and put down her cup. "I don't know. I think there's more to units than meets the eye, or more than the manufacturers intended."

"They're part-human, right? Do they seem like it?"

"Not so much as you'd notice at first. Including human neurons in their make-up is only supposed to heighten their intellectual capacity and make them somewhat autonomous, so they'll show initiative in the absence of direct orders, but I think it gives them...a kind of consciousness? Sometimes...you know, this is going to sound crazy, but sometimes I see one of them out of the corner of my eye, and I feel like it's watching me."

Idris' eyebrows rose. "Sounds creepy."

"No, I don't feel it in a menacing way. In fact, it feels comforting, like deep down they're looking out for me." She gave a short laugh. "I'm probably projecting onto them. They say people do that."

"Sorry," said Idris, "that *still* sounds kinda creepy." He looked out the canteen window. "Looks like it won't rain today, for a change. How about I show you around?"

"I'd love that," Jas said, a little too enthusiastically. "I mean, if you have time. Is this your day off?"

"I swapped a shift. We should make an effort to show our visitors a proper welcome."

There was that smile again, and the resultant tingle in Jas's stomach. "Thanks. What do you suggest we do?"

"To be honest, there's only one thing to do around here, and that's buggy riding."

"You mean drive around in those vehicles they have at the shuttle base?"

"That's right. We have a fleet ourselves. We can borrow a couple and drive out of town. Take a look around. I can show you the sights, such as they are. How does that sound?"

"Great."

It certainly was fun taking the buggies out of Dawntown

and into the surrounding landscape. The vehicles were perfect for driving over the low hills and soft vegetation. They were very easy to handle. She followed Lieutenant Theron for some way, until the town was out of sight. Then the officer slowed until she drew alongside him, and they drove on side by side, the lieutenant waving and pointing when he wanted to turn right or left. After a little while, he would get her attention only to make faces at her. Jas laughed, and the stress of the last few days began to fall away.

They drove up a long slope. Jas's vehicle slowed down as it struggled to cope with the incline. Then she crested the top, and the view made her draw a breath. She braked and stopped. A brilliant turquoise ocean stretched out on the other side. Idris was already on his way down to it, and Jas pressed the accelerator to follow him. At the ocean's edge, he stopped and got out. Jas drew up alongside. As she opened her door, the deep scent of the water hit her nostrils, and the warm breeze stirred her hair.

Driving around Dawn had been fun, but in truth there'd been little of great interest, once she'd gotten used to the deep copper tinge of the plant foliage. Nothing as specialized as flowers or trees seemed to have evolved yet on the young planet, and there was a monotony to the landscape. But this ocean was something else, and the contrast of the blue water to the native color of the plants made it seem even more vivid.

"It's breathtaking," Jas said.

"Yes," replied Idris. "It certainly is. It's a shame we didn't get here first to claim it."

"What do you mean?"

"Dawn's oceans belong to the Haidiren, except for a few

reserves they gave us when the occupation agreement was drawn up. You and I shouldn't really be in this area, near the ocean, but it's okay. No one will see us."

Jas had forgotten that humans were sharing the planet with an alien species. "How come we and the Haidiren are both colonizing this place? I've never heard of that happening before."

"Nope, and for good reason. The minute one side starts to lust after something the other side has, it's the perfect recipe for war, which is the main reason why my division is here. The Haidiren only leave the ocean to mate and reproduce, and even then they never go farther than the beaches. They had inhabited Dawn for decades before we arrived, and we'd established a colony over several years before they knew of our existence.

"Once both sides found out about each other, it was difficult to disband either colony and move out. In truth, I think the Haidiren were too mellow to push it, though it was their right as they were here first. They agreed we could have the land, which they don't use anyway, and a few small sections of ocean, providing we leave them in peace."

"Do they own this spot? Is our being here going to cause a diplomatic incident?"

Idris laughed. "The Haidiren won't tell on us. It's more my superiors who'll have something to say if someone sees us and reports us. But we drove so far out of town, we're alone here, I can guarantee it. There's no one else around for kilometers."

Jas watched the ocean. In all the worlds she'd visited, she didn't think she'd ever seen an expanse of water such a rich and striking color. She let the warm breeze permeate her skin and hair and wondered what the Haidiren looked like. All she knew was that they were aquatic. She didn't think she'd seen a picture of one.

After some time standing in silence with Idris, she noticed that his arm was around her waist. It was a nice feeling.

6

Lingiari was waiting in the lobby of the hostel when she got back that evening, long after dark, feeling better than she'd felt for a long time. She'd had a wonderful day with Idris, and talking with him about what had happened with the aliens aboard the *Galathea* had eased her conscience a little.

"Where have you been?" she asked the pilot as she came through the door.

"I was gonna ask you the same thing."

"I went to the beach. It was amazing." She was a little breathless after walking back from the army barracks.

"I was looking for you all day," said Lingiari.

"I was looking for you, too, yesterday evening and this morning. What happened to you?"

"Nothing much. I was just looking around the place, then I went to bed early and woke up late. Since then, I've just been hanging about. Looks like you had a better time than me."

"One of the soldiers took me sightseeing. Lieutenant Theron. I'll introduce you. You'll like him."

"Oh, right. Some of the crew arrived while you were gone. It looks like Haggardy's sending them down from the ship and through testing as fast as he can."

"They all passed the screening?"

"It sounds like it. No one remembers anyone arriving who they didn't see again on the other side."

"That's good. I'm waiting to see what happens when Haggardy takes his test. He hasn't arrived yet?"

"No. No sign of him anyway."

"Delaying the inevitable maybe," said Jas.

"Maybe. Have you eaten?"

"Yeah, I ate at the barracks."

"I hope you had something better than what we were served for dinner. Do you want to go out somewhere?"

"Sure," she replied, but when they asked the woman at the hostel desk where they could go, she couldn't suggest anywhere.

"Nowhere at all?" exclaimed Lingiari. "What do people do in the evening around here? Don't you have a vid center or anything like that?"

"Dawntowners stay home with their families, do close work, and pray to the Earth Mother," replied the woman, looking up at the pilot from under heavy eyebrows.

"Sounds a lot of fun," said Lingiari. He turned to Jas. "How about we go for a walk around town? I've been cooped up here all day waiting for you to come back. I need to stretch my legs."

It was dark outside, and Jas was tired from walking the beach and dunes with Idris. She also knew it was hard to navigate the streets without lights, but she said, "Okay, just for a while."

They stepped out into the night. Jas didn't need to have worried about finding their way in the dark, because Dawn's two moons were rising, and the sky was cloudless and shimmering with stars. As she looked up, she felt a familiar chill at seeing configurations that were new to her.

They walked towards the edge of Dawntown. Each street was similar to the next. All of them were deserted, and the night was silent.

"So, what's he like?" asked Lingiari after they'd walked a couple of streets without speaking.

Jas had been so lost in her thoughts, she'd almost forgotten the pilot was there. "Who?"

"This fella you were out with today. The army guy."

"He seems nice. I thought it was kind of him to show me around." Jas wondered at Lingiari's tone, which was tense. Maybe he was stressed about the whole situation. Or maybe he was missing Flux or Navigator Lee.

"You went to the beach? I didn't know there was one close by."

"We drove for kilometers, in those buggy things. Umm...Lingiari..."

But the pilot was distracted. He was peering into the darkness ahead. "Did you see someone cross the street?"

Jas followed his gaze. A dark figure was coming towards them. Skinny and coltish like the fast-growing adolescent he was, she recognized him the moment his face became distinct in the moonlight.

"It's you again," said the kid.

She recalled his name: Makey.

"You must be from the starship too," he said to Lingiari.

"Yeah," replied the pilot. "Do you two know each other?"

"Makey here was asking to join the crew," said Jas before turning to the kid. "Look, even if we had a job for you, which we don't, you're too young. You have to be twenty-one, minimum."

"Aw come on, please," said Makey. "I'll do anything. Anything you say. I have to get out of here. I'll die if I spend another day on this planet."

"Shouldn't you be home with your family, praying or something?" asked Lingiari.

"I don't believe in all that," said Makey. "My parents, my teacher, everyone, they've been lying to us. I found out. I read about many things in books we're not supposed to see. So many things they don't tell us. I've tried to explain to my friends, but no one wants to know. No one will listen. They all want to carry on believing, even when it doesn't make any sense."

Jas bit her lip. "I'm sorry, but there isn't anything we can do. You've got to go home. This isn't the kind of place where you can survive by yourself. You need your family. I know it's hard, but in a few years, when you're older, it'll be easier. If you study, you can get a job on a passing ship, or—"

"I can't study," exclaimed Makey. "Don't you understand what I'm saying? They don't teach us anything. Only about the Earth Mother, and how to farm, and that's it. There are books at school, but they're locked away. They don't give us the chance to do anything different. And whenever starships come, everyone pretends they aren't there. Please help me. You're my only hope."

"That sucks, kid, but—" said Lingiari.

"If you don't help me, I'll head out of town and carry on walking till I die. I can't go home now. Not after running off for the second time." He paused for breath, and his face twisted as if he was trying to stop himself from crying. "My Da'll beat me to death this time."

Jas's eyes widened. "Your father beats you?"

"Yes, if I'm too slow at something or say my prayers wrong. Sometimes he doesn't even have a reason."

Lingiari and Jas exchanged a look. After a moment's silence, Lingiari said, "Come with us."

Back at the hostel, Jas and the pilot sneaked Makey upstairs and into Jas's room. In the light of her single electric strip, the boy lifted his shirt. Both drew in their breath at the sight of his welts and scars. Jas winced at the memory of accompanying Idris and the other soldier as they'd taken the kid home the day before—home to receive his beating.

"I'm sorry," she said. "I didn't know."

"Do you see what I mean now?" asked Makey. "Da says he's the head of the family because that's what's natural, and he has to keep us in order. He ignores my sister, but me, he beats. I've told my teacher, but she just says a father must discipline his children. Will you help me now? If I can't get a job aboard your ship, can you smuggle me to Earth?"

7

Carl picked up a cracker from the bowl on the breakfast table and pretended to take a bite before slipping it inside his shirt. Four crackers were already secreted there. He wished there was a way to take some of the soup upstairs to Makey, too. The boy was beginning to look thin and pinched after three days hiding in Harrington's room, but the soup was impossible to transport easily, and it would look suspicious if he was seen carrying a mug of the slightly salty, mostly tasteless liquid up to his room. No one in their right mind would ask for seconds unless they were starving.

It had taken the boy's father longer than twenty-four hours to report him missing. Makey had said he was probably waiting for him to make his own way back when he got hungry enough, and he feared the shame Makey's running away for a second time would bring on the family. A man being in control of his brood was important among Dawn-town inhabitants, and his Da would lose considerable face.

Along with Harrington, Carl had bought the boy fruit and vegetables from the market and saved him a portion of his meals. But only fresh food was for sale, nothing cooked or processed, and the *Galathea's* crew had been given very little money.

If they hadn't been harboring a runaway, the cash would have been plenty. The hostel provided all meals, and there was little to buy. The amount of food they could give Makey, however, was barely enough to keep the boy going. He was constantly hungry, Carl was sure, though he never complained.

Together, he and Harrington had developed a routine to keep the kid safe. Every night, when the hostel was silent, Carl would go to Harrington's room, then check that the coast was clear. Makey would slip out and down the corridor to the shower, and either Harrington or Carl would linger outside the door to prevent one of the *Galathea's* crew from entering and spotting him.

Every evening, the ranks of shipmates at the dinner table had grown as more and more were processed and stationed on the planet to await their return to the ship. Every morning, those who knew what was going to be served up for breakfast would tease the newcomers with tales of the delicious homegrown, home-cooked meals that Dawn had to offer.

Carl did a mental count of those present. More than three-quarters of the crew had been processed. He wondered what the hostel staff would do with the rest, as all the tables were full. They would probably have to employ a shift system, which would suit Harrington and himself as, currently, they could only attend meals separately, one of them always remaining with Makey upstairs.

Someone was banging a mug on a table. The hubbub faded to a hush, and Carl turned to see who it was. Haggardy. Haggardy had arrived. He must have passed the test. So he wasn't a Shadow after all. Carl took advantage of the crowd's momentary distraction. He grabbed a handful of crackers and stuffed them in his shirt. He now had quite a bulge, so he spread them around and evened them out.

"Good morning, crew," said Haggardy. "I just wanted to say a few words, then I'll let you get back to your breakfast. I'm pleased to report that one hundred and twenty-one crew members have been tested and every single one of them has passed. Today and tomorrow, the remaining crew members will arrive from the *Galathea*. Providing the testing continues without hiccups, I anticipate we will be Earth-bound within three days, and we can all put this episode behind us."

A hand rose. "Permission to speak, sir."

"Go ahead."

"Do you mean to say we're abandoning the mission, and we won't get our bonuses?"

"Continuing the mission is out of the question." A disgruntled murmur rose from the crew. "I'm surprised anyone would think that might be the case. Captain Loba and most of the officers have died, and the *Galathea* has sustained significant damage. It's neither practicable nor safe for us to go on. However, Polestar is always interested to hear from applicants with experience aboard a prospector. You shouldn't have too much trouble finding a new berth."

Just-audible cursing sounded around the room, and cups and cutlery were slammed down. Carl understood the crew's frustration. They'd been only halfway through their mission and had only achieved break-even point for Polestar. A few more resource-rich planets would have made their jobs worthwhile. As it was, everyone had risked their lives and suffered the intense boredom and inconvenience of space travel for the wages sweat shop workers received back on Earth.

Haggardy raised his voice above the griping hum. "I was pleased to hear from the governor of Dawn that you've behaved yourselves so far. I expect your good behavior to continue for the rest of your stay. Let's be the perfect guests, eh?"

The acting master's words had little effect. The angry reaction from the crew continued. Haggardy began to make his way over to Carl, and the pilot's stomach fell. What did the man want with him?

"Lingiari, I'm surprised to see Harrington isn't with you. You two are best friends, after all, aren't you?"

"She ate already. She's up in her room. I'll go get her if you like." Carl swung his legs over the bench he was sitting on and stood up.

"No, no. No need for that. What I have to say is for both of you to hear. I'm sure you'll pass on my message. As you can see, I passed the test. I'm not a Shadow. But I am master of the *Galathea* for our passage back to Earth. I expect you both to accept that and put this nonsense behind us. I have no wish to have defense units trailing me wherever I go.

"When we board ship, you will return to your duties and your normal freedoms. However, should either of you even attempt to question or challenge my authority by word or deed, be assured that you will spend the rest of our voyage in the brig and be tried for mutiny along with Karrev and his cronies when we arrive at our destination. Is that clear?"

"As glass, mate," Carl said. He had a sudden idea. Maybe Haggardy could persuade the governor to look into some of the problems Makey had told him and Harrington about.

"You will address me as—"

"Yeah, whatever. Look, I get it, okay? You're the real Haggardy, but we've got bigger problems right now."

Haggardy's lips thinned to a line at Carl's wisecrack, and his face remained set throughout the pilot's speech.

"This place is kratted. The parents beat their kids and treat them like slaves. They're feeding them a load of BF in school and not teaching them science or maths or anything to do with technology. The poor sods don't have a chance. It's like the kratting Dark Ages around here."

"Hmpf. Have these people broken any local laws or regulations?"

"No, that's the craziest part. There's no law against hitting your kids. They say it's natural. Parents can do what the hell they like."

"Then I'm not sure what you're getting at, Lingiari. What's the problem here?"

"The problem is, no one's doing anything to protect these kids. The governor won't do anything about this stuff, so I was thinking maybe you could—"

"But if, as you say, the parents aren't breaking any laws...?"

"There's more than one kind of law, mate."

"I'm not your *mate*," said Haggardy, his eyes narrowing. "You will refer to me as Acting Master Haggardy. One more instance of insubordination from you, and I'll confine you to your room and garnish your entire mission's wages.

"I'm extremely disappointed to hear that you appear to have been interfering with the running of this colony under its governor. I order you to have nothing further to do with Dawn's inhabitants forthwith. You are to utter no statements that could be construed as critical of its people or its government, nor have any contact with anyone other than crew members of the *Galathea,* except for strictly necessary interactions.

"And you can tell Harrington the same, as no doubt she's

also been interfering with local affairs." He raised a finger and pointed at Carl. "I'm warning you, Lingiari, there's to be no offense to our hosts for the rest of our stay, or there will be severe consequences." He left without another word.

Carl went upstairs to give Harrington the bad news. She took it as well as he expected.

"The kratting misborn idiot."

Makey was sitting on Harrington's bed. Carl suspected he slept there while the security officer slept on the floor. The kid hung his head. "No one's going to help me. I told you. I'll have to go out into the wild. I just hope my Da never finds me."

"Makey," said Harrington, "you're going back to that misborn father of yours over my dead body."

"But if your captain won't do anything," said the kid, "how am I going to get away from my Da? If I can't come with you guys, I don't have anywhere else to go."

"We'll find a way, don't you worry," said Carl.

There was a knock at the door. With practiced skill, Makey got down on the floor and slid under the bed almost before the person finished knocking.

Harrington went to the door. The hostel receptionist was there. She looked from Carl to Harrington. "Someone downstairs for you. Lieutenant Theron, he says his name is." She threw another look between them and left.

A weight settled over Carl's heart at the mention of the soldier's name. But Harrington obviously liked him a lot. He wasn't going to stand in their way.

8

____

Jas met Idris outside the hostel. It was good to see him again, and it was good to get out. She'd spent long hours cooped up with Makey, worried that, if he was left alone, someone would come into her room or he would make a noise and be discovered. If he were taken back to his parents' house, there wouldn't be much anyone could do to help him.

The morning light and the sight of the lieutenant lifted her mood.

"It's good to see you again," said Idris. "Sorry I haven't been round. Since the news about that missing boy came out, we've been searching for him from sunup to sundown."

"I know. I heard about it. It's the kid you took back home the day we met, isn't it?"

"Yeah." Idris frowned. "How'd you know that?"

"I remembered his name. Makey."

"Oh right. Well, we're still searching, but I wondered if you wanted to join us? We're searching a swamp, so it won't be much fun, but...I thought we had a good time the other day..."

"I'd love to come along. Thanks for asking me."

His smile broke through his tired, drawn expression.

THEY TRAVELED in a different direction from the way to the beach. Lieutenant Theron and Jas were accompanied by three soldiers, each in a single vehicle. After traveling for an hour or so, they stopped. Jas didn't see why until she got out. The land before them looked similar to what they'd covered: vegetation of bright copper and other reddish hues, but through the plants before them, patches of water glinted that Jas had failed to spot. If they'd continued on their path, they would have driven right into the swamp.

The soldiers pulled down two boxes that had been stowed on their vehicles' roofs, and as they opened them, the interiors sprung out and began filling with air. In a short time, two dinghies lay next to the water. Oars were slotted together, and coils of rope with rubber-tipped grappling hooks were placed in the boats.

Idris grimaced. "This was a stupid idea. I don't know why I invited you to come help us drag a swamp for a dead body. It's not much of a day out. You can wait here if you'd prefer."

"No, I'd like to help."

The three soldiers got into one dinghy, and Jas and Idris got into the other. The two parties agreed to meet back at a certain time, and they set off in opposite directions. Idris rowed the dinghy out.

"We'll go to the southern edge and work our way back. If the kid did fall in here, he won't be far from shore."

The boat slid through the water easily. Idris avoided the large clumps of plants, and the rest parted smoothly.

"Do you ever come out here to fish?" Jas asked, trying to lighten the mood.

"No fish in these swamps, as far as anyone can tell. There's nothing that you would recognize as fish in the ocean either. There are some *things*, but I'm not sure what they're called. Under the agreement with the Haidiren, we aren't allowed to catch them. All we can harvest from the water on this planet is that seaweed they serve up for breakfast at the hostel."

"Urgh. Don't remind me."

Idris chuckled. "We can eat at the mess hall when we get back. I might even be able to get you some more coffee."

"That'd be great." Jas paused. She wanted to talk to the Lieutenant about Makey, but she wasn't sure how much she should tell him. If he knew that Makey was hiding out in her room, he might feel it was his duty to inform the governor. That would get her into a lot of trouble, and he'd probably feel bad. She didn't want to put him in an awkward position. But if he did know what was happening, maybe he could help.

"Idris, why do you think Makey ran away? He was crying when you took him home. Do you think he was frightened of what would happen to him there?"

"Of course he was. It's not possible to survive out in the wild here. His parents would have been mad that he'd put his life at risk and worried them so much. That's natural."

"Do you think they might have even hit him for it?"

Idris shrugged. "Maybe. Dawntowners are very religious, very strict. But I don't think they would actually hurt him. More like scare him enough to stop him from trying it again. For his own good."

"It didn't work, though, did it? If his father punished him, it didn't stop him from running away again."

"Yeah, well, you got me there."

"What do you think of Dawn, Idris? I mean, what do you think of what the people are trying to achieve here?"

"It's not my business to think anything of it, Jas. I'm just doing my job here. And when I get posted somewhere else, I'll go and do my job there."

"But you must have an opinion. You must have noticed how ignorant the children are. The kind of nonsense they believe in. I mean, do you know what goes on in their schools? What they're being taught?"

Idris stopped rowing and looked strangely at Jas. She clamped her lips and turned to gaze over the water. She'd said too much. How would she know what was taught in the schools unless a certain kid had told her? After a moment, Idris picked up the oars again and continued rowing. They didn't speak again for a few minutes until the boat bumped against a bank. "We're here. Let's start dredging. Do you want to row or throw?"

"I'll take a turn with the oars," Jas said.

They swapped seats, and Jas took the oars from Idris. He sat in the bow and threw a rope, hook first, into the water, which swallowed it. He pulled hand over hand on the rope until the hook appeared at the side of the dinghy, covered in foul-smelling, rust-colored slime. He threw it three or four times more in different directions.

Jas pulled on the oars and maneuvered the boat a little farther along the bank, where Idris threw the rope again.

She regretted her words, which seemed to have killed the good feeling between her and the lieutenant. While waiting for Idris to drag the water, she looked out over the swamp again. Once you got used to the red hues of the vegetation, Dawn wasn't an unattractive place. In every similar waterlogged location she'd been to on Earth, such as in the

U.K. and Chile, the strongest repellent didn't deter the ravening insect life. But on Dawn, she hadn't seen a single fly, wasp, mosquito, or other flying annoyance, not even in this swamp.

Complex life had its downsides, and as a young planet, Dawn had none of them.

Then she saw it. Sticking out in the dark, rusty red swamp vegetation, was a patch of green. It stood out so boldly against the copper, she didn't understand why she hadn't seen it before.

She almost dropped the oars. She realized why she hadn't noticed the green thing. It was moving. It was alive, and it had popped into view.

Idris followed her gaze. "Don't move. Stay still, or you'll scare it."

"What is it?" Jas whispered.

"Haidiren. You can talk normally. They can't hear, or if they can, speaking-level noise doesn't bother them. But don't move. They're very sensitive to movement. It'll pick up the movement of the boat in the water, even at this distance."

"I thought they lived out in the ocean."

"They can live anywhere there's water."

"What's it doing?"

"I've only seen them twice before, and each time they were...yes...there it goes."

The green patch in the distance blurred and seemed to shake. It grew larger, and copper patches appeared. Jas realized it was the vegetation behind the creature showing through it. The creature was coming apart. It was breaking into many pieces, and the pieces were spreading out and slipping into the water.

Jas's hand rose to her mouth. In all her years of visiting

alien planets and seeing extraterrestrial life forms, she'd never witnessed anything quite like it. One minute the Haidiren was an individual, solid body, and the next, it had dissolved into thousands of parts.

"Is it dying?" asked Jas.

"No, it's reproducing. After fertilization, it breaks into segments, and each segment grows into a new Haidiren. That's what I read somewhere, anyway."

"That's amazing."

"Yeah, it is," agreed Idris, pulling the final length of rope up as the last piece of Haidiren disappeared. "We can go now."

The sight of the Haidiren broke the tension that had formed between Jas and Idris. As she rowed the boat back to their starting place, they chatted and laughed about all the things they'd seen throughout their travels. It turned out they'd visited some of the same planets, and they traded tales of encountering weird and wonderful life forms.

When they got back, the three soldiers were waiting for them. Their efforts to dredge the swamp had also drawn a blank, of course.

"We had no luck, either," said Jas.

"Yeah, strange that," said Idris in a mildly sarcastic tone.

Jas looked away.

At the army base, she took the opportunity to fill her belly. The food was only average, but compared to everything else Dawntown had to offer, it was delicious. And, true to his word, Idris worked his charm with the kitchen staff and brought her a steaming mug of heaven.

After they'd walked back to the hostel, they said goodbye, then there was an awkward pause. Idris went to kiss her. Jas didn't resist, and she returned the kiss.

Idris was a good kisser, but something had gone wrong somewhere out on the swamp. She wasn't sure what it was, but despite their growing closeness, the spark of her feeling for the lieutenant was no longer burning as bright as it had been.

9

———

It had been easy to evade the humans' tests. Since its creation in a far distant place, the Shadow had lived among the humans, mimicking their ways, until it had been sent with its group to the new world. These new arrivals were not tested. They were the protectors of humans, the fighters, and they were not suspected because they did not come from planets where Shadows had been found.

It had walked the new planet. It had found a place near to the humans' habitation; not so close that the humans quickly noticed, but close enough to bring victims there. It had made the connection, and over time, the trap had grown.

When it was complete, the Shadow selected its first victim. It had needed to act quickly. There was another of its kind in the space vessel orbiting the planet that risked detection if it was forced to submit to the tests.

It had selected a human in authority—a human with control over the others. After she had been replicated, her Shadow would be able to command others to accompany her to the trap. The victim had not gone willingly when she saw where the Shadow was taking her, but it had forced her.

Now, on the other side, in the void, signals entered. Information. Coding of a life form. The human's data flowed in. Chemicals, functions, processes, systems—the tiny messages communicated all they needed to know. What was used to create the human, what was left unused, what waited in the background to be activated.

In the physical world, the human was forced farther in. She would be unable to escape.

In the otherworld, the information that was used to create and maintain her during her brief life—the merest flicker compared to time in the ether—was examined, interpreted, decoded, and finally the blueprint, the map of all that made up the human's physical body, was comprehended.

Next came assimilation.

Everything that made up the human's knowledge, experience, memories, and personality was contained within her physical form. Her nervous system held the information. Capturing the human, disintegrating, assimilating, and interpreting her nerves and brain told all there was to know. The data was complete, and the replication process could begin.

Pushing through into another reality was a great struggle. Worse was becoming separate from the whole. Cut off from the communal mind, the thing forced itself through the barrier. Rivers of fire ran through its new body as it contacted air, temperature, solidity, gravity, and pressure. Its partly formed mouth gaped silently. Skin took color, organs differentiated, and blood permeated newly created capillaries, veins, and arteries. The heart contracted jerkily once, twice, and began to pump.

Senses came online. Nerves transmitted signals about light, sound, touch, balance, position, and smell to the brain. Fired by activity, the brain grew aware. Memories flashed up. Items of knowledge. Feelings. Associations. A lifetime's experience within a few seconds.

The creature breathed. It felt. It knew. It moved. Another Shadow was born.

Time to find more humans.

10

Carl was at the window in Harrington's room.

"Jas told me not to open the shutter," said Makey. He was sitting on her bed. None of the windows in Dawntown had glass, and Carl had wondered if it was because it was 'unnatural'. They had wooden shutters made of rows of slats that were angled up to capture sunlight, which meant it was impossible to see out of a window without opening the shutter. Carl had opened it the minute he'd heard Harrington's and the army officer's voices below as they returned from their day out.

His stomach twisted painfully as he saw the two of them kiss. His interest in Harrington, which had once been something quite shallow and physical, had grown over the time they'd spent together fighting the growing menace of the Shadows. He wasn't sure yet what it had grown into. He couldn't put a name to how he felt when he thought about her, but certain situations brought those unnameable feelings strongly to the foreground—situations such as seeing her kiss another man.

"Jas said we mustn't open the shutter," repeated Makey, louder.

Carl closed it and turned his back on the window. *Jas.* Even the kid got to call her Jas. He always called her by her surname, like they were just shipmates, not even friends, and she'd never told him otherwise.

"Is something wrong?" asked Makey.

"No, everything's okay. *Jas* is back. She should be here in a few minutes." Carl sat down and stared, unseeing, at his hands. The few minutes Harrington was taking to say goodbye to the lieutenant seemed to be an awfully long time. Like a child picking at a scab, he imagined what she could be doing that was taking so long.

Finally, the gentle, coded knock sounded at the door. Carl opened it and let the security officer in. Her lips seemed more full and red than usual, and her hair was a little messy.

"Guess what I brought," she said as soon as the door was closed. From a satchel at her side she pulled out some rolls with a pale yellow, creamy filling. "They let me take a bag home from the canteen."

"What are they?" asked Makey as she handed him and Carl a roll each.

"Cheese rolls."

Carl's eyebrows rose. "Real cheese?"

"No, it's cheese spread, but it's pretty good."

Makey was sniffing his roll. "What's cheese? And what's wrong with this cracker? It's too thick, and it's soft."

"It isn't a cracker. It's bread, which is made of flour and yeast. And cheese comes from milk, which comes from cows."

"Urgh," exclaimed Makey. "I remember now. I read about cheese. That's disgusting. Why would anyone want to eat something that came out of an animal's breast?" He handed his roll to Carl, his upper lip twisted in disgust.

"Try it, mate. You might like it." Carl held out the roll to the boy.

Makey folded his arms. "No way. I never heard of anything so revolting in all my life. Except maybe people actually eating dead animals. Can you believe some people did that?"

"Huh, some people still do," said Carl. When the teenager's arms remained stubbornly folded, he went on, "You know, if you want to travel the galaxy, you're gonna have to get used to eating a lot weirder things than cheese rolls. You won't be able to pick and choose when you're eating aboard a starship. You take what you're given and act grateful for it."

This wasn't strictly true. In Carl's experience, the quality of food aboard prospecting ships wasn't too bad. Eating was one of the few things to break the monotony, and even stingy companies like Polestar recognized the benefits of keeping a crew well-fed. But a little white lie wouldn't hurt. The kid needed to toughen up a bit if, by some miracle, they managed to get him aboard the *Galathea*.

Sighing, the boy held out his hand for the offered roll. He took a tiny bite and grimaced at the taste. Taking a larger bite, he chewed mechanically, a look of extreme suffering on his face. Harrington stifled a snort of laughter, and for a moment Carl forgot what he'd seen her doing with the lieutenant. He began to laugh, too, and soon Makey joined in as he was stuffing the rest of the roll into his mouth, trying to get the ordeal over with quickly and nearly choking in the process.

Someone ran down the corridor outside. Carl put his finger to his lips and mouthed *Shhh* to the other two. They couldn't risk someone hearing a stranger's laugh coming from Jas's room. With a chastened look, Harrington immediately clammed up, and the kid wasn't slow to follow.

In a soft voice, the security officer said, "Sorry, you're right, Lingiari. We can't attract any attention, especially after today."

"Why? What happened?" asked Carl.

"I went with Idris to dredge a swamp, looking for your body," replied Harrington, turning her gaze to Makey. His cheery young face dropped.

Idris, thought Carl.

Harrington shook her head. "I think I said too much. I think he guessed that I know where you are. He might even have concluded you must be here. He isn't stupid, and it isn't like I'd know anywhere else to hide you around here."

"Krat. What did you say?" Carl asked.

"It was innocent enough. I was just talking about the school system here, but how would I know about it? The Dawntowners don't speak to offworlders, and they don't let their children speak to us, in case we corrupt them I suppose, so how would I know about their education? It isn't like they advertize the curriculum."

Makey's face was stricken and pale. "I can't go back home. I can't. My Da'll kill me this time. I know it."

Harrington sat beside him and put a hand on his arm. "I'm not going to let them take you back home. But I realized there's something we haven't thought of. Is there another family you could stay with? A family who'll treat you more kindly?"

The boy shook his head. "My Da's very important. There's no one who'll stand up to him. They wouldn't want to make him feel ashamed of not being able to bring up his own children."

"There's nothing for it, then," said Harrington. "We've got to get you aboard the *Galathea.*"

"I dunno how that's going to happen," said Lingiari. "I didn't have time to tell you this morning, but Haggardy's here."

"He passed the test? He isn't a Shadow?"

"He passed the same test as us, so..." He shrugged. "I spoke to him about the situation...just generally. I didn't tell him about Makey. Guess what he said. You know what he's like."

"'We can't interfere.'"

Carl nodded.

"Kratting misborn idiot. You know, I'd almost prefer it if he was a Shadow. At least he'd have an excuse then."

Makey looked from Harrington to Carl. "Isn't there anything you can do to persuade your captain? I know I don't know anything about working on a starship, but I'm strong, I'm a hard worker, and I learn quickly."

"If you weren't a minor, and if it weren't Haggardy we were talking about," said Carl, "you might've had a chance. But—"

"We have to take him, Lingiari," said Harrington. "And you know how to do it."

"I do?"

"You smuggled Flux aboard the *Galathea*, didn't you?"

"Yeah, but, in case you hadn't noticed..." He gestured toward the boy. "He's a little bit bigger."

"Come on, you know about shuttlecraft. Can't you think of *anywhere* we could hide him when we return to the ship?"

Carl frowned. He did know the shuttle model they used on Dawn. He knew it well. Maybe there was a space you could squeeze a skinny kid in. "But it isn't just hiding him on the shuttle, is it? We've got to get him through security at the shuttle base first."

"So let's go to the base and check it out," Harrington said. "Security's my thing."

Despite his hurt feelings about the security officer, Carl's heart warmed. This was what he liked about her—when she had to do something that really mattered, she never gave up.

"Okay. Let's go tomorrow."

Makey clenched his hands into triumphant fists, grinned, and said a quiet, "Yes."

"All right. Goodnight, then," said Carl, and went to leave.

"Wait a minute, Lingiari. Do you think Makey could sleep in your room tonight? This floor's killing my back."

After a pause, Carl replied, "Sure. I'll just check that the coast's clear." He looked into the corridor, trying not to think about why Harrington might really want her room to herself.

11

Jas didn't dare approach Idris for help getting to the shuttle base. He wouldn't take long to guess she was up to something that had to do with Makey, and after their time in the swamp, she wasn't sure how he would react. It seemed like he didn't really care about what was happening on Dawn. He wasn't a bad person, but it was just another job to him.

She and Lingiari returned to the Dawntown parking bay to find the single-seater vehicles they'd used to come into town. Several of them were there, and they were unlocked. It made sense that no one would be worried they might be stolen. The vehicles were programmed to travel only between town and the base, and no one would have any reason to go there unless they were leaving the planet.

Jas and Lingiari had thought up a flimsy excuse for their visit. It wouldn't hold much water, but they couldn't think of anything better, and there was at least a touch of credibility to it. They got into vehicles, and they were soon on their way out of town.

As they approached the base, a shuttle swooped out of

the sky, glinting in the sunlight. The shuttle sped like a dart to its destination, slowing quickly as it neared the base. Some more crew members from the *Galathea* were arriving to be tested.

Jas wondered if Karrev and the other prisoners in the brig would come that day. She also wondered how they would test Lee when she couldn't leave her stasis chamber. She hoped the navigator had been okay without her and Lingiari to look out for her.

Most of the crew members had been processed, which meant Jas and Lingiari had only a couple of days at most to figure out how to get Makey off the planet. If they could just get him aboard the ship, they would have few problems hiding him during the trip back to Earth. Once there, things might get a little tricky for him, but illegals arrived all the time, and it was too expensive to send them home. Plus, Makey was a minor. He'd probably spend a year or two in a government home before starting a new life.

Jas's vehicle stopped outside the shuttle base entrance. She got out and went with Lingiari to the door, where two guards stood. They showed the guards their ID. "Is the governor here? Could we speak to her?" As she spoke, prickles ran down Jas's back. Something was wrong.

She looked closely at the guard she was speaking to. He seemed ordinary enough, but something bothered her about him. Without answering her, the other guard spoke into a comm console at the desk. The governor's voice replied, telling him to escort them to her office.

The room and the governor looked the same as they had when Jas had arrived. Nothing *seemed* to have changed, but something had. The security officer and pilot sat down.

"You aren't scheduled to depart today," said Governor Siam. "Is there something I can help you with?"

"We wanted to ask a favor," said Jas. "Lingiari here and I, well, we've been impressed with how smoothly the process of vetting the crew has gone. There hasn't been a single hitch. We were wondering if we could have a look behind the scenes to see how you do things around here. You know I'm chief security officer and Lingiari's the pilot on the *Galathea*? We'd like to see if there's anything we could learn."

The governor frowned. She didn't answer for a moment, and her eyes became unfocused, then she blinked, as if remembering where she was. "You'd like to look around the base? That won't be a problem. We have nothing to hide here."

She told the guard, who was waiting at the door, to take Jas and Lingiari on a tour. It would have been better if they'd been able to snoop alone, but that was too much to expect.

The place was small. It included a modest shuttle landing pad, lobby, four testing rooms, a holding hall, a waiting room, the governor's office, a meeting room, guard-rooms, and a cargo bay for imported goods arriving from Earth and elsewhere. Jas made a mental map of the place: the fastest route to the shuttle, the number of guards, and what weapons they had. She wondered how the guards might be distracted or diverted.

The problem was, the shuttle base was so bare and open. Like Dawntown, the place was minimalist. No screens, nooks, or crannies to sneak a stowaway behind or into, and taking him across the field to the shuttle without being seen would be impossible.

Lingiari spotted the shuttle pilot who had brought them to Dawn, and he went to talk to the woman. She looked upset for some reason, but Lingiari quickly engaged her in a conversation about the shuttle model she flew, clearly refreshing his memory about the interior of the craft.

To Jas's great surprise, the woman suddenly broke off what she was saying and burst into tears, throwing her arms around an astounded Lingiari. At the same moment, a familiar figure burst from one of the testing rooms. It was the man who had tested her. He stumbled out, his hands over his face. "I can't take it anymore. I just can't take it," he muttered.

Then Jas felt it too: overwhelming sadness. It was a feeling of hopelessness and despair, as if she were utterly lost and would never be happy again. She took a deep breath and tried to think through her emotions. This wasn't her. This was coming from something else—something that projected its emotions onto others. She went through the open door of the testing room, and there they were.

The large fungal creatures she'd named Paths had been brought to Dawn for testing. It was inevitable. Jas had found them on the very same planet where the Shadows had put their traps. Of course. They were under suspicion of being Shadows themselves. She was only surprised that the scientists knew how to test these creatures. It meant they knew about them. Even Jas, who had studied hundreds of alien species during her training and since, hadn't known about Paths. She didn't even know what they were really called.

She suspected the testers didn't know Paths as well as they thought they did, judging from the scientist's evacuation of the testing room. She choked back a sob and approached the strange creatures. They seemed to recognize her, because her intense sadness and anxiety reduced and was slowly replaced with relief and happiness.

"It's okay," she said. Did they understand her? If not, maybe they would get the gist of what she was saying.

Maybe they could read others' emotions as well as transmit their own. "They've only brought you here to test you. You'll go back up to the ship soon. Then we'll be on our way." As she spoke, an idea occurred to her. The Paths, as she'd noticed when she'd brought them to the *Galathea* were hollow.

Another emotion began to grow in Jas. She felt uneasy and watchful, as if something bad was going to happen, but she didn't know what. The emotion was an echo of how she'd felt in the lobby when they arrived. "You feel it too, do you?" she asked the Paths. "I'm not crazy, then." But she knew she wasn't crazy. Though she had no explanation for her precognition of impending danger, the sense had never failed her.

"What was that about?" asked Lingiari as he joined her, having extricated himself from the sobbing shuttle pilot. "I feel terrible. Oh, I get it. It's those things. You weren't kidding about them, were you." The Paths had been stored in quarantine, far from human contact aboard the *Galathea* after Jas had explained their strange ability. It was Lingiari's first close encounter with them.

"No, I wasn't. They seem to be feeling a bit better now."

"They were upset about being taken from the ship?"

"Yeah, I think so."

A crease formed between Lingiari's eyebrows. "But they're not over it, right? Or...I'm getting that they feel kinda..."

"Scared. They're feeling worried and scared."

"What do they have to be scared about?"

Jas replied, "That's what I'd like to know." But she already had an idea. An idea based on the behavior of the governor. The woman had seemed almost the same, but not quite. That look, that lack of focus—Jas thought she'd seen it before. She'd seen it in the *Galathea's* dead master, Loba, in the geo-phys scientist, Margret, and in the officers who'd been forced into the Shadow traps. Was the governor the same person she'd been when they'd first arrived? Or was she a Shadow?

12

———————

Jas couldn't sleep that night. If the Shadows had invaded Dawn, everyone on the planet was at risk. But she had no proof, and without it, maybe no one would believe her, not even Lingiari. There was certainly no point in telling Haggardy of her suspicions. He wouldn't take any action even if he believed her. If he was interested in anything other than saving his own skin, he would have acted aboard the *Galathea*.

There was also still the chance that he wasn't the real Haggardy. The testing protocols must have failed and allowed Shadows onto the planet, either from the *Galathea* or another ship. If the tests were faulty, they could have let a Shadow Haggardy through, and any other Shadows that had arrived with him.

The governor had seemed normal when they'd arrived, and the Shadows seemed to go for the highest in command as soon as they could. Maybe she'd been the first victim. On the *Galathea,* the second person taken had been Master Loba, and the Shadows' process from that point had been to herd the next lowest in the hierarchy into a trap.

She sat up. A trap. If the Shadows had invaded, there had to be a trap somewhere on Dawn. It would be undeniable evidence.

As the predawn light filtered through the slats in her window shutters, Jas made her plan. She would try to find the Shadow trap. If she found it, she would take Makey and whoever else she could and waste no time getting off the planet.

The kid had slept in Lingiari's room. After breakfast, she brought him some of her crackers and took over from the pilot, who stepped out to stretch his legs. The boy chewed glumly on his poor meal. He was thin and pale from the lack of sunshine and proper food, but his confinement would soon be over, one way or another.

"Makey," said Jas, "have you traveled much outside your parents' land?"

"Yes, we have to," replied the kid. "Every Tenthday, we have to go out alone into the wild areas so we can commune with nature and give thanks to Earth Mother. Well, that's what we're supposed to do. I wander around until it's time to go home. It's Tenthday tomorrow, in fact."

"When you were walking around, did you notice any buildings? Apart from the ones in Dawntown, I mean?"

"No. How could there be buildings out there? Why would anyone make a house in the middle of nowhere?"

"These wouldn't be like a house. They would be shaped like hexagons—six-sided rooms grouped together, making up a building. And they're dark gray and low to the ground. No windows, just a few doors in the same shape, and nothing inside."

"Oh, you mean the Haidiren house," said Makey. "Yeah, a few of the kids have seen that. It's way out of town, next to a river. They must have built it fast, because it wasn't there until recently. I first saw it the Tenthday before last. It looks just like you say." He frowned. "I didn't go inside. We have to keep away from the Haidiren, and they have to keep away from us. It's the law."

"It's lucky that you and the other kids kept your distance. Makey, I don't think that's a Haidiren house. I think it's something much more dangerous."

His eyes widened. "Like what?"

"I'll explain later. But for now I have to go and find it, to check if it's what I think it is. Can you give me directions?"

"Yes, but, I've been thinking about things. Jas, I'm not sure I want to leave Dawn."

"What?"

The kid hung his head. "I keep thinking about my sister and my mam. If I leave, I might never see them again. And they'd be alone with Da. I feel like I should do something to protect them."

"I know that feeling, Makey, and it's understandable that you feel that way. But you're very young. These things aren't your responsibility. It's up to the people of Dawntown to fix problems like your dad's behavior."

"But they won't. I've tried telling people. They don't want to hear me, or they don't care. I don't know what else I can do. But running away doesn't seem right either."

"I'm sorry. I don't have the answer for you. Only you can decide that for yourself. But if you want to come with us, I don't think you should feel bad about it. And I'll do everything I can to help you."

"All right. Thanks, and thanks for everything you've done for me."

Jas smiled. "No problem. Now, can you tell me how to get to that building?"

Makey's knowledge of the surrounding landscape was

detailed, due no doubt to his many years of wandering. Jas memorized the instructions he gave. It was in an area of the Dawntown surroundings she'd never been to before, was way out of town, and she needed a fast way to get there. Only one person would be able to help her.

IDRIS SMILED, a little coldly, Jas thought, as he came to meet her outside the base.

"It's good to see you," he said. "I came over yesterday morning, but you'd gone out. I thought you might want to join us in the search for that kid again."

"Yeah, sorry, I went to the shuttle base. A little reconnaissance." Maybe he was upset that she hadn't spent one of her last few days on the planet with him, but she couldn't help that.

"The shuttle base?" He looked puzzled, but he didn't take it further. "So...?"

"So I'd like to join you in the search today, but I've got somewhere in mind you might want to look. I have directions."

"You do? I don't see why not. Come on, let's go."

They borrowed two vehicles from the army compound.

Makey's directions were very good. He'd described the landmarks to watch out for accurately, and after a while, they came in sight of a fast river. They left their vehicles and walked north along the bank, where the ground was rocky. The rocks were large and sharp-edged, as if from a landslide that had occurred not very long ago.

"Do you know where we're going?" asked Idris as they scrambled over the boulders.

Jas replied, "I heard there's a building out here."

"A building? What kind of building?"

"Idris, I know it might sound crazy, but if this building is what I think it is, the whole colony is in danger. You'll have to believe what I tell you and help get everyone out."

"Let's see what we find."

The color of the walls of the Shadow trap were nearly the same as the surrounding rock, as if the thing were trying to camouflage itself. Jas almost didn't see it, but it didn't match the irregularity of the natural rock, and its perfectly symmetrical form soon became apparent. She grabbed Idris' arm and pointed the place out to him.

There was no doubt in her mind now. The trap was exactly like the ones on K. 67092d. One or more Shadows had arrived on Dawn, and now their trap was catching the populace and releasing more of its kind into the world. What the Shadows' aim was, she still had no idea, but she didn't need to know.

"That's it, Idris. It's a Shadow trap. They were all over the planet we were on before we came here, and they captured and killed our master and about twenty of our officers. Have you heard of Shadows? That's what they were screening us for at the shuttle base."

The lieutenant began to climb over rocks, heading toward the trap.

"No, don't go in there," exclaimed Jas. "Don't touch it, Idris!"

But the man ignored her. He approached the dark hexagonal entrance. Jas raced to catch up to him. In her hurry, she slipped and gashed her knee on a rock, smashing her elbow at the same time. Painful vibrations ran up her arm and into her shoulder. "Idris, please, listen to me. Please." She got up and clambered over the rocks.

The lieutenant was nearly there. As he lifted a foot to

step inside, Jas threw herself at him. She grabbed his thighs, making him fall. He lay face downward in the dirt, half inside the structure's entrance.

"Come on, Idris, get out of there. It's dangerous." She let go of the lieutenant and stood up. He turned over. As Jas met the man's gaze, she gasped. His face was blank. Idris was gone.

He was a Shadow.

She turned to run, but she wasn't fast enough. His hand fastened around her ankle. She fell down, jarring her bloody knee. The Shadow began to drag her toward the trap. Jas's fingers scrabbled to grab a hold of the bare soil. She kicked to free her leg, but the Shadow's grip was like a vice.

Giving a grunt, Jas drove the heel of her other foot into its head. The kick would have knocked out Idris, but it had no effect on the Shadow. Slowly, inexorably, it pulled her inside.

13

Makey held the shutter open just a crack. It was wide enough for him to see out, but no one outside who happened to be looking up would recognize him. He was alone. Jas had gone out to find that weird building he'd seen by the river. Why it was so important, he didn't know. The spacewoman hadn't said. Carl was downstairs eating lunch. Makey's stomach rumbled. He hoped the pilot would bring him up something to eat soon. He was starving. He'd been hungry ever since he'd run away, but he didn't like to complain.

The pilot had explained that morning that they had to try to smuggle him aboard the shuttle, and what he had to do when he arrived on the ship, so that no one would find him. If he followed their instructions to the letter, Carl had said, he would be able to travel aboard the *Galathea* on its return to Earth. What would happen there, Makey wasn't sure.

Carl had also said something about how he shouldn't tell anyone that he was conceived and born naturally, with no 'modding', and that he should tell people as little as possible about his background, or he might find it hard to get a place at college, or a job. These problems had baffled Makey, though he hadn't said so because he didn't want to seem ignorant. In truth, he was very ignorant, he knew, but that was the least of his problems.

The problem was, Makey still wasn't sure he wanted to go. He hadn't said anything to Carl, but the idea that he was running out on his sister and mother had continued to grow. As well as that, he felt like leaving all the problems of Dawntown behind him wasn't right. There was more than he'd told anyone about—some things that he had only just begun to put together in his mind, or was it that he was finally admitting them to himself? Things like people going missing. People who questioned what was happening on Dawn.

Leaving was cowardly. Jas and Carl didn't quit when things got hard. They'd said it would be difficult to get him onto their ship, but they were going to try anyway. They didn't just give up and walk away, like he was doing.

He watched the people in the street. Most were crew of the *Galathea*, but some were his own people—Dawntowners, going to and from the market or their farms and houses. His heart was heavy as he recognized people that he had grown up around. If he left aboard the starship, he might never see Neeve or Mam again. If he left without letting them know that he was alive, it would break both their hearts. He was sure of that. They had to think he was dead by now.

What had they done to deserve such treatment from him? Nothing at all. Neither his sister nor his mother had shown him anything but loving-kindness all their lives.

Dawntown was busy because it was Tenthday, and after the Celebration, the town would empty as the Dawntowners went into the surrounding landscape to commune with Earth Mother.

Earth Mother was something Makey had never understood. Earth was thousands of light years away, according to the library books. Why would Earth Mother be there on Dawn? Shouldn't she be looking after her own planet? His Da had said that Earth Mother was the guiding spirit for the entire universe. Makey had thought that maybe she should have a different name if that were the case, but he hadn't dared contradict his father. He wondered if there was a Dawn Mother, but he'd never felt her spirit enter him on Tenthday any more than Earth Mother's, as was supposed to happen.

He rubbed his eyes with the heels of his hands. He would not cry. He would not. He was nearly an adult now. He would not blub like a little child at its mother's skirt. But he was behaving like a child. He was running away from his problems instead of fixing them.

A very familiar figure appeared in the street. It was Neeve, going to Celebration Hall. He opened the shutter wide. His decision was made. He would not leave her alone. He didn't care anymore what happened.

"Neeve," he called. "Neeve, I'm up here."

Plenty of people turned and looked toward him, but his sister didn't seem to hear. In another moment, she was gone.

Behind Makey, the door opened.

"Krat, what are you doing, mate?" Carl was back from lunch. He ran across the room to the window and pulled the shutter closed. But he was too late. Dawntowners and the starship crew members in the street were staring up at the window, wide-eyed.

Carl grabbed his shoulders and spun him round. "What

are you thinking, kid? We told you to be careful not to let anyone see you."

"I know," replied Makey. "I'm sorry, Carl, but I realized something. I can't go. I can't leave my family. At least not without trying to change things around here. If I run away, everything's going to carry on the same. My mam and sister will think I'm dead, and Neeve's going to grow up just as ignorant as me.

"Everyone's going to continue to recite their Earth Mother prayers when anything goes wrong, and assume that if She doesn't put it right it's because they aren't devout enough. It's wrong, Carl. If they want to believe that, they can, but they can't bring their children up in ignorance. It isn't fair to them. They should be able to choose for themselves."

Carl put his hands on his hips. "You're not wrong. Or at least, I agree with you about educating the kids properly. But what can you do about it? If you go back to your family, from what you've told us, your life'll be in danger. I think it's better if you come with us, or you'll never have another chance to leave."

The footsteps of many people sounded on the stairs, and a loud knocking came from the door. Carl quickly locked it. "Open up," shouted a voice. "We know you've got Makey in there. You've been hiding him."

"I want to talk to them. I want to try to get them to see sense," said Makey.

The knocking sounded again, louder. The doorknob twisted forcefully, and the door rattled in its frame. "Open up. We're taking that boy back to his family." More footsteps sounded on the stairs.

"It's Tenthday," said Makey. "Soon, everyone'll be at

Celebration Hall before they go out to pray to Earth Mother. I can talk to them there."

A key was inserted in the lock, forcing the other out. The hostel receptionist must have brought a spare. The door flew open, and several Dawntowners fell into the room in their haste to get to Makey.

He backed into a corner, and Carl stood in front of him, his arms folded across his chest.

"Get out of the way," said a Dawntowner to Carl as he strode up to within a few centimeters of the pilot. "This is none of your business, offworlder."

"The kid just wants to talk," replied Carl. "He wants to go to your Celebration."

"We're taking him back to his family, where he belongs."

"No, he's got a right to be heard," said Carl.

"He's a kid. Get out of the way, or you'll regret it."

The pilot's back was toward Makey, and he looked around the man's shoulder at the angry Dawntowners in dismay. He worried what the Dawntowners might do to Carl.

"You can't take him," said the pilot. "Go and get your governor. She can sort this out."

In answer, a burly Dawntowner swung a fist at Carl, who ducked and struck back, hitting the man in the throat. As he staggered away, two Dawntowners stepped forward to take his place. Carl dodged a punch from one of them, but the other hit him square on the side of his head. The pilot staggered.

Makey couldn't let Carl get hurt on his account. He would have to try to find another way to fix the problems on Dawn. He stepped around the man. "I'll come with you," he said to the Dawntowners. "I'll go home."

"No, Makey," said Carl, shaking his head as if to clear it. "You can't give up."

Turning sad eyes to the man who had sheltered him and become a friend over the last few days, Makey allowed the Dawntown men to grab him and pull him toward the door. "It's all right, Carl. I'm not giving up, but I'll go with them for now."

"Makey, no," shouted Carl.

The Dawntowners formed a huddle around him and led him out of the room and down the hostel stairs. But at the bottom, crew members of the *Galathea* were crowded, drawn by the disturbance. They filled the hallway as they watched Makey and the men making their way down.

Carl's voice sounded from above. He was standing at the banister rail. "Stop those men, shipmates," he called. "That kid's been hiding here because his dad beats him, and they're taking him home for another beating."

The Dawntowners' grips on Makey's arms tightened and they drew closer, crushing him between them.

"Is that right, kid?" asked one of the *Galathea's* crew.

"No," replied a Dawntowner. "We don't beat our kids round here. That's a lie."

"I wanna hear what the boy says," said the crew member who had spoken. The rest of them closed ranks at the bottom of the stairs, forming a mass that was difficult for the Dawntowners to penetrate.

Makey held his breath. He didn't want a fight. He didn't want more people to get hurt. But he was tired of pretending. He exhaled. "It's true."

At his words, the *Galathea* crew pushed up the stairs, forcing the huddled Dawntowners back. The struggle was brief but decisive. Makey found himself quickly extracted and lifted bodily over the shoulders of men and women, away from the people of Dawntown. As they set him down, a man asked, "Where do you want to go, lad?"

"I want to go to Celebration Hall."

He was free, for the moment. What the future held for him would become clear in the next few hours.

14

———

Jas let the bloody rock fall from her numb fingers.

It wasn't Idris.

She couldn't take her eyes from the oozing mess that was all that remained of the Shadow's head. His black hair was red, coated in glistening blood. Off-white bone shards poked out, and his brain protruded through his crushed skull. His eyes, framed by their long lashes, stared, unmoving. He looked surprised at this sudden accident; this unanticipated shift from life to death. The lips she'd kissed only the day before last were parted.

As she crouched over the body, Jas reminded herself that it had been him or her. He'd been trying to get her into the Shadow trap, or die in the attempt. She'd had no choice.

It wasn't Idris.

Jas wished that she could cry, but she could not.

She blinked as she returned to an awareness of her surroundings. All was quiet but for the rush of the river. How long had they fought? She didn't know, but the sun didn't seem much farther across the sky than it had when they'd arrived at the river. They might have been fighting for only a few minutes, though it had seemed like ages.

The Shadow who looked like Idris had been stronger than her, and it had assimilated Idris' army training. If it hadn't been for the rock that she had accidentally brushed with her hand, he would probably have won, and right now she would be experiencing the same fate as the unlucky lieutenant.

Had he gone into the structure looking for Makey, not knowing what it was? Or had he been taken there in the way that Margret had taken Loba? Whatever had happened to him, it meant that there was already an unknown number of Shadows on Dawn.

The thought brought her up, shuddering, to a higher level of self-awareness. Pain emanated from her elbow and knee where she'd fallen on the rocks earlier, and it was joined by a severe ache in her shoulder where the Shadow had forced her arm behind her back. She also became aware that her face was wet. She wiped the wetness, and her hand came away covered in blood. Her forehead was cut, and she had a bloody nose. But none of her bones were broken. She'd been worse off after a fight.

Jas stood up unsteadily. Keeping her eyes averted from the prone form at her feet—*It wasn't Idris*—she looked around to get her bearings. She had to follow the river to return to the vehicles. She would take one back to Dawntown, though how she would explain why she'd returned without the lieutenant, she didn't know. Neither did she know how to explain to the Dawntowners what the structure was, or that the soldier she'd killed was actually an alien.

Did they know what Shadows were? She had a feeling the governor had never told them why starship crews sometimes came to the planet, or if she had, she guessed that the locals were so welded to their willful ignorance that they refused to acknowledge the fact of the Shadows' existence.

She began to climb across the rocks, heading toward the river. She didn't take a last look at the structure—*It wasn't....*

There was no doubt in her mind that Dawn was compromised, and every single person on the planet was under suspicion of being a Shadow.

She reached her vehicle quickly, slipped inside, and started it up. On her way back to Dawntown, she tried to figure out what she would say when she arrived, but she couldn't come up with anything. She would just have to play it by ear. She had to urge Haggardy to return the *Galathea's* crew to the starship immediately, and hope that none of them had been taken victim. Dawn's method of vetting for Shadows was obviously flawed. The testers had either failed to spot one among her shipmates, or they'd let one through from another ship, and it had built or triggered the formation of the trap.

Jas pulled up a short distance from the army base and left the vehicle there. She couldn't risk any of the soldiers seeing her and asking why she was alone and injured, or what had happened to Lieutenant Idris Theron. Her throat felt swollen. What had happened to him? She still didn't know exactly what went on inside the structures. Whatever it was, she hoped it had been quick.

She walked into town. The streets were quiet. She thought the Dawntowners must have been out on their nature trek, or whatever it was that Makey had called it. But when she arrived back at the hostel, she was surprised to find that it was also nearly empty. The place had been crowded with most of the crew of the *Galathea* that morning, but only Haggardy was there, with a few of his cronies in the canteen. He was just the man she needed to see.

The former first mate lifted a sardonic eyebrow as she limped toward him.

"Been scrapping again, Harrington? I swear you seek out trouble like a moth seeks oblivion in an open flame. You should be careful. It'll be your downfall one day."

Jas pulled out a chair and sat down heavily. She winced and straightened her injured leg with her hands, easing it under the table. "Shadows are here, Haggardy. You have to get the crew off the planet."

His upper lip curled. "That's ridiculous. We've all been tested. If there's one place in the galaxy there are no Shadows, it's here."

She'd known he would resist, but he would have to act. He would have to do something decisive, even if it would rock the boat and cause his superiors difficulties. The man's attitude made her blood boil, but she wouldn't let her anger master her self-control. Shouting at him would get her nowhere. She rested her elbows on the table and leaned forward. Haggardy leaned perceptibly back. Jas was pleased that her bloody face alarmed him. It might make him easier to persuade.

"Acting Master Haggardy," she began, and the man smiled a little at this unusual display of deference from Jas, "if you want, I can take you, and you, and you," she nodded at the two newly appointed officers sitting on either side of him, "right now, to a Shadow trap. It isn't far from here. About an hour by vehicle. At its entrance lies a body in the form of former Lieutenant Theron, who was stationed at the barracks here."

She swallowed before continuing, "Haggardy, I know your opinion of me isn't high, but do you really think I would kill another human being for no reason whatsoever? Do you really think I would murder someone in cold blood? The Shadow of Lieutenant Theron was determined to drag me into that trap, and he died trying."

Her gaze shifted to the woman and man with Haggardy. She had to trust that, if Haggardy was a Shadow, these two were not. "Do you want me to take you there and prove it to you? The longer we stay on this planet, the greater the risk that someone in the crew will get enticed or forced into the trap, and then that person will come aboard the *Galathea*. If we take him or her to Earth, the Shadows will spread there."

"Why should we take your word for it?" asked the woman.

"Come with me now if you don't believe me. Look, we have to leave soon anyway. Just bring the time forward. Though I have a feeling that Governor Siam might not be keen to let us go."

"Why? Are you saying the governor's a Shadow too?" the woman asked.

Jas nodded. "On K. 67092d, the first opportunity they had, the Shadows went for the person in command, Loba. Here, that would be the governor." Haggardy's cronies looked troubled, and the old man himself was frowning. She straightened up and looked around the canteen. "Where is everyone?"

"Hmpf, you noticed, finally?" said Haggardy. "Your little interference in local affairs has come to light."

A chill settled on Jas's heart.

"That young friend of yours," continued the acting master, "the Dawntowner you've been hiding from his family, he was discovered."

Jas half rose from her seat. "Where is he?"

"I believe he's gone somewhere they call Celebration

Hall. Apparently, he wants to tell the townsfolk his story. Let's hope it's a good one."

Jas was already limping out of the canteen. *Celebration Hall.* She knew it. It was the only three-story building in town. The kid must've made up his mind to stay, but what would his dad do to him? Rubbing the crusted blood from her face, Jas set off in the direction of Celebration Hall.

By the time she got there, the meeting was nearly over.

15

———

Makey's footsteps faltered along with his resolve as he made his way to Celebration Hall. Having Carl alongside him helped bolster his confidence a little, but the prospect of confronting Da and speaking out against everything he'd been taught since he was a babe suddenly seemed a lot harder than it had when he'd been hiding in the hostel.

Just a few days' absence from his home, school, and his Da's fields had made his life on Dawn less real to him. His mind had been among the stars and planets for a while, anticipating the exciting adventures he would have when he got aboard the starship with the help of his new friends.

At that moment, as he walked the familiar streets of Dawntown, drawing alarmed glances from latecomers to Celebration Hall prayers, he felt he was still very much on his home planet, and that he would probably never have any other life.

"Buck up," said Carl, who was walking next to him. "Your dad might not come. He might be out looking for you still."

"Oh, he'll be there. Da would never miss prayers. He leads them."

"The father that beats his kids is the prayer leader? Is he the head of your religion around here?"

"Not in name. Earth Mother is the head, if there is one. No one is supposed to tell anyone else what to do, but a lot of Dawntowners look up to Da. He has plenty to say on what is and isn't natural, and that kind of thing. Quite a few of my friends' parents go to him for advice if they aren't sure what they should or shouldn't use, or how the people in their families should behave, or what it's okay to speak to their children about."

"Are you there when your dad's talking with these people?"

"Oh no. Me and Neeve are supposed to be asleep, but our house is small, and Da's voice is loud."

"Sounds like he won't take it well if you criticize his opinions in front of the rest of Dawntown?"

"That he won't."

Carl clapped him on the shoulder. "I'll be there with you, Makey. Say what you've gotta say, then we'll get out of there, right? What's the worst that could happen?"

Makey didn't share the pilot's optimism. He didn't know about the Dawntowners who had gone out to commune with Earth Mother on a Tenthday and had gotten lost, or who supposedly couldn't cope with the tough life and had 'unnaturally' walked out into the sea and drowned. And he didn't know that it was the more outspoken in the community that this had happened to; those who had questioned the Dawntowners' ways. He could hardly breathe when he thought of what he was about to do, but he knew the time for hiding the truth was over.

Celebration Hall was at the end of the street.

Word of Makey's arrival had gone before him. Before he even reached the door to Celebration Hall, Da came striding out. In all his years of witnessing his father's many angry outbursts, he had never seen such fury twist the man's features. Makey stopped, and his legs refused to move another step. Da marched toward him. Makey's head shrank into his shoulders as memories of the beatings he'd received surfaced.

A shadow fell across him. Carl had stepped protectively in front.

"Get out of the way," growled Da. "No one gets between me and mine. Move now, or you'll find out what Dawntowners do to offworlders who don't obey our laws."

"I'm not going anywhere, mate. Not until this kid has a chance to have his say."

"He isn't an adult. He has no right to address the prayer assembly. He can do that when he's eighteen," said Da. "If he makes it to eighteen," he added in a lower tone.

Makey glanced up and caught the black look his father was giving him around the side of the pilot. He remembered the punch Carl had received on his behalf back at the hostel. His resolve began to melt. "Maybe I should go with my da, Carl. I'm sorry I dragged you and Jas into my troubles."

"Good," said Da. "Get over here, Makey. You can apologize to everyone in Celebration Hall for your stupidity, then I'm taking you home."

"Hold on," said Carl, turning to face Makey. He put his hands on his shoulders. "Is this what you want?"

Makey looked into the man's broad, honest features. He couldn't lie to him. "It isn't, but what can I do? You can't help me. It's just the two of us against the rest of them. I'll have to find another way."

"Just us two?" asked Carl. He held out a hand toward Celebration Hall.

Makey had been so focused on the terrifying spectacle of his furious father, he hadn't noticed that scores of the *Galathea's* crew had accompanied them and were lounging against the building's walls. As he gazed at them in surprise, a man gave him a thumbs up. The sight of the men and women from the starship injected him with strength. Like air into the lungs of a drowning man, new resolve flushed through Makey.

He swallowed to stop his voice from quaking, and addressed his father. "I'm going to speak to them, Da. I'm going to speak to the Dawntowners, and there's nothing you can do to stop me."

Carl stepped out of his way. Setting his shoulders, Makey brushed past his open-mouthed father. He strode into Celebration Hall. His da didn't follow.

Inside, watchers who had been lurking at the windows scrambled to the benches, and the loud hum of outraged opinions quietened. By the time he reached the podium, a tense silence had fallen save for the crying of a tired, hungry baby, which was soon quelled by its mother's breast.

Makey touched the sides of the lectern. It had been brought from Earth, he'd heard, and it was made of a material called wood, which came from plants called trees. Trees grew almost mythically tall, according to what he'd read in the school books. A faint hope stirred in his heart that he might one day see a tree.

He'd never for a second dreamed he would ever stand there. Now that he had his chance, finally, to speak to them all and try to put right some of the things that were wrong, he didn't know what to say.

His gaze roved over the audience's expectant faces. He

knew every single person there, either well or by sight. They were all familiar to him. His nervousness fell away. Good or bad, these were his people, and they always would be. That was where he could start.

"I'm one of you," he said. "I've spent all my life on Dawn, working in the fields, going to school, growing up with my family. I've learned and obeyed the rules, said the prayers, communed with Earth Mother. I've done all of it, the same as everyone here. But today I have to tell you that what we're doing isn't right."

He told the audience what it was like being a child on Dawn. He talked about knowing that he was being kept in ignorance, about never being allowed to question anything, about being hungry and cold, about seeing people who he'd loved die without any treatment but prayers. He explained how lost and hopeless he felt because he had no choice in his life; that he was slave to another person's idea of what was right and wrong in the world.

Seventeen years of frustration and unhappiness poured from Makey's heart and mouth. Some of the audience covered their faces and wept. Others frowned. A few got up and stormed out, but most remained in their seats, still and silent, listening. Several seemed to only stare.

Finally, an older man in the audience stood and pointed at Makey accusingly. "That's enough. You sit down and be silent. You've no right to speak to us. What do you know? You never lived on Earth, where half the population is out of their minds on drugs. Have *you* seen first-hand what they did to that planet? The heat and pollution? The destruction?

"What do you know about what your da and the rest of us went through to bring you here? What do *you* know about how we suffered to give you a new and better life? You children are pure. You have the chance to live a natural life, the way you're supposed to. You've no right to criticize things you don't understand. You should be grateful for all we and Earth Mother have done for you."

"Hey," came a voice from the doorway. The lanky form of the pilot lounged there. Jas had arrived, too. "Do you know what his dad does to him?" asked Carl. "Is that the kind of thing your Earth Mother would want?"

"Stay out of this, offworlder," replied the man. "This is none of your business. Go back to your drink and myth."

"When parents beat their kids, I make it my business," said Carl.

"Don't you dare start spreading lies about this boy's father," said the man. "His Da's one of the best of us."

"You sure about that?" asked Carl. "Show them, Makey. Go on."

He didn't want to show them. His father's harsh treatment of him wasn't what this was supposed to be about. Though Da's punishments were bad, there was so much more wrong with how his friends were being raised on Dawn. But the audience was staring. They wanted to know the truth.

Makey quickly turned his back to them and pulled his shirt over his shoulders. The marks of his most recent beating had faded somewhat, but silvery lines marked the evidence of what his father had done to him over the years.

Shocked cries and gasps came from the audience. The baby began crying again, but it was ignored by its mother. The previously silent weeping became audible sobs. Makey pulled down his shirt and faced the audience once more. The older man who had spoken slumped into his seat, his hand over his eyes.

Someone gripped his arm. Carl had come over. "I think you've said enough, mate. That's given them plenty to think about. Look, Harrington's saying Dawntown's in danger. If you want to come aboard the *Galathea*, you've gotta leave with us, now."

But Makey wanted to see his mother and Neeve. He'd spotted them at the back of the room. After explaining to Carl, he made his way over. The audience was breaking up. People were standing and leaving or huddling in groups to talk. A few Dawntowners approached to speak to him, but Makey pushed past them.

When he found his mam and sister still in their seats, he rushed toward them, but his steps slowed. They were looking at him, but they didn't come over to meet him, or even react. Were they angry at him for running away and letting them think he was dead? They didn't seem angry. Their expressions were kind of blank.

"Mam?" Makey squatted at his mother's feet and peered into her face. Something wasn't right. "Neeve?" he said, turning to his sister.

"Makey," said a voice behind him. It was Jas. "Makey, you need to come away."

He stood to face the spacewoman. "No, I've decided. I'm staying here, with my family."

"Yes, you need to come with us," his mam said.

Except... He looked into the woman's eyes. Something made him recoil. He stepped back, bumping into Jas.

"Come with me, Makey, and I'll explain," Jas said.

"No, come with us," said Mam.

"Yes, come with us," said Neeve.

"I...I..."

"Makey, do you trust me?" asked Jas.

"Yes, I do."

"Then come with me now. These aren't your mother and sister."

At Jas's words, the two women rose and grabbed at him. Horror clawing his throat, Makey backed away and fought them off with Jas's help. He forced his way through the crowd and toward the door.

"Dawntowners," shouted Jas as she came with him. "Listen to me. You're all in great danger. Please, listen. There are Shadows among you."

16

Jas put an arm around Makey's shoulders as they returned quickly to the hostel. The kid had done well, really well. He'd stood up to his abusive father —stood up for what he believed in. But he'd also begun to understand that his mother and sister were dead.

Word from Haggardy had arrived just behind her when she got to Celebration Hall. She'd hardly been able to believe it, but the man had listened to her and ordered an immediate evacuation of the *Galathea's* crew. And not a moment too soon. The presence of Shadows among the audience at Makey's speech meant the situation was already dire.

She'd explained to the Dawntowners the threat that faced them. At her words, Makey's mother and sister had bolted, but she still wasn't sure the town's inhabitants completely believed her. At least they had begun to look questioningly at each other, maybe trying to discern who was a Shadow and who wasn't. At least they hadn't started praying to Earth Mother to solve their problems.

She'd done what she could, but now they had to get

back to the ship. And they had to take a certain young man with them.

"You did a great job," she said to Makey.

"No, I didn't. If I'd done a great job, my mam and sister would be going with us."

"I'm sorry for what happened to them."

"You're sure it wasn't them?" the kid asked.

"What do you think? Was that your mother and sister back there?"

Makey looked down and slowly shook his head. "Dawn isn't safe anymore, is it? What are these Shadows?"

Jas sighed. "I don't have time to explain properly, but you're right, Dawntowners are in danger. But that doesn't mean you shouldn't come with us. When we get back to Earth, you can be an advocate for Dawn and convince the Global Government that they need to send out more forces to protect the inhabitants. When the Shadows have been driven out, the government can investigate what's been going on here."

Makey's expression remained troubled.

When they got back to the hostel, all was in turmoil. Men and women were crowding the lobby and stairs, carrying their ship's bags over their shoulders. A full-scale departure was in progress. Upstairs, the doors in the corridors were open, and the remaining crew of the *Galathea* could be seen inside packing their belongings.

They found Haggardy in his room. He'd wrangled himself a large, airy space with a view of the coppery countryside rather than the street. He was folding his spare uniform carefully to put it away in his master's suitcase. The man blinked at the sight of Jas and Lingiari and young Makey.

"Hmpf. If you're here to ask me what I think you want to

ask me, the answer is no. Lingiari, I was wondering where you'd got to. You're to report to the shuttle base immediately."

"Hagg...Acting Master Haggardy," said Jas, "this young man's planet is under attack from hostile aliens. He has a right to asylum under Global Government law. You can't...you would be well-advised not to—"

The corner of Haggardy's lip lifted. He stepped close to Jas and peered with mock concern into her eyes. "Are you feeling quite right, Harrington? These recent displays of proper deference and civility are quite out of character for you. Perhaps you've picked up a virus?" He moved back to his case. "Is this the real Harrington? Or are you a Shadow?" He laughed at his own joke before pointing at Lingiari. "You. Shuttle base. Now." He resumed his packing.

"I'm going," replied Lingiari. As he turned to leave, he gave Jas the smallest hint of a wink. He wasn't going anywhere until they figured out a way to get Makey on board the *Galathea*.

Jas remained where she was and folded her arms over her chest.

Haggardy sighed. "Harrington, the entire population is under threat. Are you suggesting we take *all* of them with us? If we can't take them all, who should we take? Which ones? It seems to me that if we're to take anyone it shouldn't be strong, fit Dawntowners who can fight to protect their colony, like this young man. We should be taking the very old and the very young, the ill and disabled. If you think I'm going to try to explain to the Global Government why I brought him and no one else, you have another think coming."

"Well, you know, that would be a great idea," Jas replied. "Let's take those too."

The acting master paused as he pushed his clothes into his case. "The *Galathea* is a commercial vessel. We are not supposed to interfere in military affairs. Dawn has a fully equipped and staffed military base. We must let them handle it. Our duty is to Polestar's investors. We must return their vessel to Earth along with as many samples of planetary resources as we can take. And that is as far as our responsibilities extend." He snapped his case closed.

"Why am I even explaining this to you? The answer is no. Escort that boy to the street and make ready to leave. The *Galathea* needs her chief security officer." His suitcase in one hand, he went past Jas and into the corridor.

"What the hell are *you* doing still here?" Jas heard Haggardy shout.

"Just going to pack, sir," replied Lingiari, from outside. He'd ignored Haggardy's order and was lingering about.

Jas smiled. Lingiari had a way of not following orders that was far more subtle—and probably far more effective—than hers.

"Get down that shuttle bay immediately," said Haggardy. "It turns out they have two shuttles but only one pilot. We can double the speed of the evacuation with you flying the spare."

Lingiari came in a moment after Haggardy stomped away.

"Did you hear what he said?" asked Lingiari, his eyes sparkling.

"Something about them having two shuttles, and..." Jas laughed as she realized what he meant. Two shuttles, and Lingiari would be flying one. She hugged the pilot and the young man. "Makey, you're coming with us."

17

———

Haggardy was right. The *Galathea* did need her security officer. And where Jas was needed right then was on Dawn, protecting her crew. She wouldn't be leaving until she was sure every last one of them was off the planet.

Lingiari and Makey had left for the shuttle base, and the hostel was emptying fast. She doubted Haggardy had taken any measures to ensure that everyone had heard the evacuation order. There could be crew members anywhere in Dawntown.

She had to check the whole place, but walking all the streets would take forever. She remembered the vehicle she'd parked a short distance from the army base. A memory of Idris surfaced, but she forced it away.

Jas jogged through the streets of Dawntown, heading for the vehicle, hoping it was still there. The streets were unusually crowded. Her warning about the Shadows, and Makey's speech and the revelation of his father's abuse had left them disturbed and confused. They were wandering the marketplace and surrounding streets.

The vehicle was exactly where she'd left it, which was unsurprising as it was 'unnatural' and no Dawntowner would have gone near it. Slipping into the seat, she started it up. She would begin her sweep at one end of town and work her way across. It shouldn't take long. Dawntown was barely bigger than a village.

At the town edges, there were few people. The single-story, earth-colored buildings had their doors and shutters closed, and the streets were mostly empty. Jas drew nearer to the town center and saw more pedestrians, but she was confident they were all Dawntowners. She knew the *Galathea's* crew, and they were relatively easy to spot anyway. Few had exchanged their uniforms for the cooler Dawntown clothes. Only a handful had 'gone native' as Jas had. She would need to keep a careful watch for those.

At the marketplace, the crowd had increased since she'd passed through only a short while earlier. As Jas approached in the vehicle, the Dawntowners drew aside with looks of disgust at the machine. She didn't mind. It made it easier to pass through them. But the amount of people meant she couldn't see everyone properly. She stopped and got out for a closer look.

She towered above the Dawntowners. Cupping her hands around her mouth, she called, "Are there any of the *Galathea's* crew here? You must go to the shuttle base immediately. We're evacuating and returning to ship."

The crowd stared, but no one responded.

"Dawntowners, do you know of any *Galathea* crew members who are still in the town?"

A hand rose. "One of yours went off that way," called a man's voice. The hand pointed.

"Thanks," called Jas. She climbed into the vehicle and drove over to the alley the man had indicated. When she got there, it was too narrow for the vehicle, so she got out and continued on foot. A Dawntowner and *Galathea* crew member were heading toward the far end of the alley, hand in hand.

"Hey you," shouted Jas, "we're evacuating. You have to go to the shuttle base, now."

The man stopped and looked over his shoulder at her, but the woman urged him on, tugging at him.

"Come back," called Jas. The man hesitated. Jas began to run over to speak to him face to face. The woman whispered in his ear. He remained where he was, indecisive. Jas got closer, and the woman continued to urge him away. Finally, the man made his choice. With a laugh, he went with the woman and ran away from Jas.

Krat. What was he thinking? Surely he didn't want to stay on Dawn? Why was the woman dragging him away?

Unless...

Jas began to sprint. Running, stumbling, and laughing, the man couldn't match Jas's pace, no matter how much the woman pulled him. The security officer soon caught up with them. The man fell down, giggling and clutching his stomach. He was clearly on a run, indulging in something he'd brought down from the ship. *Misborn.* Had he introduced the Dawntowner to his drug? No, the woman was sober as she stood over him. Her eyes were steel. Her eyes. Then the mask came down.

"Gotta go..." gasped the man, trying to speak through his guffaws, "gotta go out there, for a bit of...y'know...won't be long. I'll make it to the shuttle base. Don't worry."

Jas followed the man's eyes to the undulating landscape at the end of the alley. She couldn't see more than a narrow slice of it, but she knew what was out there. She knew where the woman had been taking him.

"Won't be long," the woman said. "Come on." She grasped the man's hand and tried to pull him to his feet.

"Let go of him," said Jas quietly.

The woman tried to pout, but she did a terrible job, as if the Shadow that had taken her was attempting to act in a way entirely at odds with the dead person's character. "Leave us alone," she said. "This has nothing to do with you."

"Let go of him, or I'll make you," said Jas. "I know what you are."

Something in Jas's face brought the man abruptly back to reality. He slipped his hand from the Shadow's grasp and edged away. As the Shadow and Jas stood looking at each other, unblinking, he stood and straightened his pants.

"I'll...I'll come with you, C.S.O. Harrington," he said.

The words were barely out of the man's mouth before the Shadow was on Jas. She was so fast that she caught Jas by surprise and knocked her flat on her back, leaving her breathless and dazed. Before she could react, the Shadow was on top of her, kneeling on her arms and grasping her throat.

Jas wrenched her body to and fro, trying to throw the Shadow off, but she was remarkably strong. But by twisting her arms, she managed to work them free of the Shadow's weight. It knelt on her chest. Jas, too, fastened her hands around her opponent's neck, and squeezed.

Drawing in a painful breath, she fought against the closing grip on her throat. The Shadow's face was deep purple, and she realized hers must be the same. Black patches appeared before her eyes, blocking her view. The creature's eyes bulged, bloodshot. Gathering the last of her strength before she lost consciousness, Jas forced her grip tighter. Something in the Shadow's throat buckled and collapsed.

Suddenly, Jas could breathe. The Shadow's grip was loosening. The bulging eyes rolled upward, and then it fell to one side, unconscious or dead. Jas lay still as she caught her breath and her sight slowly returned. The sky above was an amazing, beautiful blue.

Her shipmate's face appeared in her view. "Are you all right?"

Jas reached up to her throat. It felt okay, only very sore, and it would no doubt bruise deeply later. "Yes, I'm all right."

"More than can be said for her," he said, scratching his head. "And to think, just a few minutes ago, we were…"

Turning, Jas saw the Shadow, unmoving and lifeless, looking exactly like a woman who had been strangled to death. She turned back and sat up, wondering if she was going to be sick. "I'm sorry," she said to the man, "but she wasn't what she seemed."

"So she was a Shadow?" asked the man. "The testers told us about them. I would never have believed it if I hadn't seen one."

"I'm very sorry," Jas repeated.

"You don't have anything to be sorry for. You saved my life."

"What I mean is, it might have looked like a Dawn-towner, but it wasn't. It wasn't…"

"Look," said the man, laying a hand on Jas's shoulder, "don't beat yourself up. It wasn't a Dawntowner. That's clear as day."

18

J as put the man in the vehicle she'd left at the entrance to the alley, telling him she would get transportation somewhere else when she'd finished her sweep of the city. She jogged the remaining streets, but found no one else who should have been returning to the *Galathea*. Back at the hostel, she found the place empty except for the receptionist, who scowled at her sourly.

She ran upstairs to her room, threw her things into a bag, and raced down to the street. When she got to the parking bay for the vehicles that went to the shuttle base, there were none there.

Never mind, she thought, she could jog to the base. She could probably do it in less than a couple of hours. She adjusted her bag so that it was as comfortable as she could get it, and set off down the road out of town.

She settled into a fast jog as she left the outskirts of Dawntown behind, not sorry to put the place behind her. Would the Shadow governor of Dawn try to prevent the crew of the *Galathea* from leaving? But no, every so often, up above against the blue sky, silver glints marked the paths of the two shuttles as they flew up and down. The evacuation was going on in earnest.

Maybe Haggardy had had the good sense to keep the reason for their sudden departure secret. If the governor was a Shadow, and if he let on to her that he knew what was happening on Dawn, she would do everything in her power to prevent him from informing the Global Government.

She had no doubt that Lingiari would manage to smuggle Makey aboard the *Galathea*. They'd borrowed a spare uniform from a crew member. In the general confusion, it shouldn't be hard to slip the young man onto a shuttle.

About halfway to the base, Jas began to feel the pace. She was forced to slow down. She'd brought no water, and Dawn's warm, humid atmosphere made it hard to run. She was beginning to notice even the mild inclines of the rolling hills, and she wondered how far she still had to go, hoping it was only the ten or so kilometers she'd estimated. Reassuring herself that she still had plenty of time, she went on.

By the time she'd run another five kilometers, she was jogging barely faster than walking pace. She didn't know the time, but she'd been running for longer than two hours. Long months aboard ship had left her out of shape, despite regular training, and the lack of water was affecting her badly. She was determined to make it to the shuttle base, though, no matter what. She had to.

The first sign she had that she was drawing near was the sound of shooting. In Dawn's silence, the noise was unmistakable. Jas reduced her pace to a slow walk. Who was fighting? The crew of the *Galathea* didn't have any weapons. Was the governor trying to prevent them from leaving? Jas didn't have any weapons either, and her defense units were currently orbiting the planet aboard ship.

The sound of firing grew louder, until finally Jas crested a hill and saw the battle. A mixture of Dawntowners and soldiers—all had to be Shadows—had encircled the base. A shuttle was on the ground, and Jas's shipmates were running to it under fire. Return fire was coming from the buildings. Soldiers were the only people with weapons on Dawn. It seemed that the Shadows and humans had divided into two camps. The Shadows were trying to prevent her shipmates from leaving, and the remaining soldiers were defending them.

And the Shadows lay between her and her only way off the planet.

She watched the battle. The shuttle that was being fired upon took off. Was Lingiari flying it? Her stomach twisted at the thought that while she'd been running, the pilot had been risking his life ferrying the crew to the ship. What she wouldn't give to get a weapon and break the ranks of the Shadows to lend him a hand.

What was she thinking? Of course she could do that. There were armed Shadows right in front of her, and they wouldn't be expecting an attack from the rear. She scanned around for a rock or branch, but neither was to be seen, only the thick, moss-like vegetation. She would have to make do with what she had.

Some quiet scouting found her a lone Shadow. It was a private. He'd gotten himself a nice vantage point over-looking the shuttle base where he could shoot without being easily seen from below. Unfortunately for him, he was easily seen from behind.

A shuttle could be heard flying overhead as Jas made her way toward the man. He was lying flat on his belly, his head peeking over the rise. The soft moss adding extra stealth to her steps, she crept up behind the soldier and swung her bag at his head. The bag was too light and soft to do any real damage, but the moment's distraction it caused him resulted in his weapon in Jas's hands. She pointed it at his face. He was on his back, and she was standing over him, her finger on the trigger.

But as the man stared into her eyes, she froze. It was Trip, the private who had been with Idris the first time they'd met. And she was about to shoot him in the face at point blank range.

Except it wasn't Trip. It was a Shadow, she told herself, and it had been trying to kill her friends. But despite its soulless gaze, she hesitated. Twice, she tried to force her finger to press, and twice she failed. A weird smile began to form on the Shadow's face, and it moved slightly upward. Its movement broke the spell. This time, the Shadow would die.

Excruciating pain seared her side. She'd been shot. She fell to her knees and began to topple to the ground. Another Shadow ran toward her to take the finishing shot. She glimpsed a dark figure approaching.

She waited for the end, but it didn't come. As the Shadow soldier looked upward, its face melted in a flash of laser fire.

The shuttle noise was very loud. Too loud. She raised her eyes to see it was right above her, and Makey was hanging out an open door, a weapon in hand and grinning. As the craft descended, Trip's Shadow took off. The shuttle landed, the heat of its exhaust shimmering the air. Through the open door, she saw Lingiari lean back and say in his Australian drawl,

"Can I give you a lift?"

19

T he first thing Jas did after boarding the *Galathea* was to find some water. She took Makey with her to the canteen. She was exhausted, but after she'd dealt with her dehydration, she had to find out what was happening aboard the ship.

Lingiari had disappeared, so she went with Makey through the ship's corridors. Disorder reigned. Some of the crew had been injured in the attack of the Shadows as they evacuated, and they were making their way slowly to the medical center. Others were hauling their belongings back to their cabins or hanging around discussing their escape. No one seemed to be telling them what they should do or what would happen next.

There didn't seem much point in hiding Makey. He told her that plenty of the crew had noticed him at the shuttle base, despite his wearing a Polestar uniform. Jas worried that someone would tell Haggardy, and he might order the kid to return to Dawn before they left the planet's orbit. But a funny thing happened as they passed by the *Galathea's* shipmates. They all greeted Jas, but though Makey was plain to see, they acted like he wasn't there. She had a feeling that this selective blindness would continue for the trip back to Earth.

She put the kid in Margret's old cabin and explained to him how the bunk screen worked. She left him staring in open-mouthed wonder at the treasures the ship's database held for a kid starved of information all his life.

The Paths had been brought back before the evacuation, Jas was relieved to discover, and they'd been returned to a remote corner of the *Galathea* where no one would be influenced by their emotional telepathy.

Next stop was the stasis chamber. She'd expected to find Lingiari there, but he wasn't. Only Navigator Lee occupied the room, looking exactly as she had when Jas had last seen her. It hardly seemed possible, considering all that had passed in the few days since she'd left for Dawn.

The navigator appeared overjoyed to hear that she was back, though the stasis' synthetic voice carried no emotional inflections.

"How have you been while we were away?" asked Jas.

"I've been okay. Flux has been keeping me company, though we ran out of conversation after a while. There's only so much you can say about how to catch cockroaches."

Jas laughed. "Talking of Flux, has Lingiari been in to see you yet? I've lost track of him."

"No, Carl hasn't been here. Is he all right?"

"Yeah, I think so," replied Jas, but she began to worry. What had happened to the pilot? She'd barely finished the thought before his lanky figure appeared in the doorway.

"There you are," said Jas. "Where have you been?"

"I had to take the shuttle back to Dawn."

"You what?" she exclaimed. "Why did you do that?"

"It's not our shuttle. I had to return it. I went to pick up their pilot. She flew me up here then took the shuttle back."

"What..?" Jas had no words to finish the sentence. The idea that Lingiari could have been killed while flying back to Dawn was too strong. Memories of the deaths of the last few hours flooded into her mind and began to overwhelm her.

Lee was very interested to hear what had happened on Dawn, and all about the Shadow invasion. Lingiari filled her in. She wondered aloud how the scientists could test for Shadows, and how one had passed the test and infiltrated the planet.

"Do you think it came from our ship?" she asked.

"Who knows?" answered Lingiari. "I suppose it could've come from another ship that was sent there before us. No one said anything about previous ship's crews they'd tested. But the Shadows seemed to appear not long after we arrived." He turned to Jas, who'd been silent all through the discussion. "What do you think, Harrington?"

Jas couldn't answer. She could only look at the pilot.

"Are you all right?" he asked.

"I killed him."

Lingiari put a hand on her arm. "Who?"

"Idris. I killed Idris."

"You didn't, Jas," said Lingiari. "He was a Shadow."

"I know, but that isn't how it feels."

The pilot didn't answer, but took her in his arms.

"That's their power," said Lee, oblivious to what was happening in the room. "That's the hold they have over us. Nothing's as dangerous as the enemy you can't recognize, except the one you don't want to kill."

Lingiari lifted Jas's chin to look into her eyes. She

wanted to cry, but the tears wouldn't come. It helped that she was in Carl's arms.

"If the Shadow that infected Dawn did come from our ship," said Lee, "that means it might have returned with the rest of the crew."

"Prepare to starjump," came a voice over the comm system. It was Haggardy. They were going home.

For the moment, at least, they had escaped.

JAS'S STORY CONTINUES IN...

SHADOWRISE
Shadows of the Void Book 4
&
THE EARTH CHRONICLES
Shadows of the Void Books 4 - 7

Sign up to my reader group for a free copy of *Starbound*, the Shadows of the Void prequel that tells the story of what happened to Jas Harrington in Antarctica, and for exclusive notice of new releases, advanced reader opportunities and other interesting stuff:

https://jjgreenauthor.com/free-books/

(I won't send spam or pass on your details to a third party.)

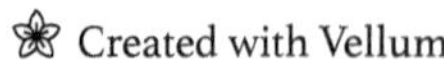 Created with Vellum

www.ingramcontent.com/pod-product-compliance
Lightning Source LLC
Chambersburg PA
CBHW070446170726
48291CB00005B/1618